DEATH AND PAPA Noël

A FOLLET VALLEY MYSTERY

IAN MOORE

Farrago

First published in 2022 by Farrago,
an imprint of Duckworth Books Ltd
1 Golden Court, Richmond, TW9 1EU, United Kingdom
www.farragobooks.com

Print ISBN: 9781788424257
Ebook ISBN: 9781788424240

Cover design and illustration by Patrick Knowles

For Father Christmas,
you do a grand job.

Chapter One

Richard Ainsworth put the lid back on his yellow highlighter. He needed peace and quiet to finish his Christmas paperwork, and the unexpected return of Valérie d'Orçay to the Follet Valley was giving him anything *but* that. In fact, she seemed to him to be on something of a mission. He carefully closed *French Tax for Dummies*, laid the highlighter neatly on top and took a deep breath.

'Well?' She was in full-on badgering mode, and Richard was determined *not* to be badgered. She wasn't even supposed to be in rural France, having told him that she had 'urgent' business in Paris over Christmas. This meant, to Richard at least, that some poor sap was going to be tracked down at great expense and delivered to whoever her paymasters were this time. Probably all wrapped up too. Presumably, even bounty hunters have a festive streak in them. However, keeping track of her in the few months they'd known each other had proved futile; she would turn up when least expected and disappear when most needed. So, for now, he was resigned to having her almost like a tidal presence in his life and, whether going in or out, destabilising the sand beneath his feet. 'Well?' she repeated.

'Well what?'

He was fully aware that this type of non-committal response was akin to lighting Valérie's fuse and sending her mood rocketing from level one to ten in mere seconds, but Richard had come to a decision; he was not going to commit to anything any more. The only thing he was going to commit to was the decision to bow out from all commitment. It felt to him that he had spent the vast majority of his adult life being tossed about by other people's whims, like a beachball by a group of performing seals. Well, if that was going to happen when he put effort into life, it was going to happen when he didn't. So he had decided to go full *Casablanca* Humphrey Bogart and was now 'sticking his neck out for nobody'.

Take Valérie, for instance, and their, for want of a looser term, 'relationship'. He was aware that he was behaving like a lovestruck teenager. Or, worse, a needy puppy, though lower in the pecking order than her actual dog, the terminally judgemental chihuahua Passepartout. It was time to play hard to get in his opinion. Were they in a relationship? No. Were they going to be in a relationship? He had no idea. Was he divorced? No. Was he going to be divorced? Probably, though he'd left that up to Clare. He was definitely single, however. Well, single-ish. Whatever was about to happen, with Valérie or just life in general, this was his first Christmas alone and he'd been secretly looking forward to it. He had plans. Finally, he could do the things that he wanted to do over the festive period; finally, he had control.

'Are you sulking because it's your first Christmas without Clare?'

It was terrifying how she could just riffle through the messy drawers of his mind and know exactly what he was thinking. *He* didn't even know what he was thinking half of the time; the woman was a sorceress. He tried to clear his mind and picked up his tax book again.

'I just fancied a quiet Christmas, that's all. I've shut the *chambre d'hôte*, Madame Tablier is away at her sister's place on the other side of the world—'

'The next village!' Valérie snorted.

'The next village, yes. And I have a mountain of paperwork to do. It's the end of the tax year...' He lifted the book to illustrate his point.

'But the *chambre d'hôte* is not closed, Richard, because we are staying here!' She pointed towards Passepartout on the other side of the room, asleep in a bed so bejewelled and ornate that it looked more like a throne.

'Yes, but you're, well... erm...' He sighed heavily. 'You haven't even booked!'

'Do I need to?' She smiled warmly at him and he could feel himself blushing.

'Obviously not, but I thought you were staying in Paris for Christmas, anyway?'

Her response was immediate. 'Pah!' she said and started to pace the room. 'I do not like Paris at

Christmas any more. There are the smiling, happy faces reflected in the shop windows, and yet people starve and sleep in the doorways at night. It's vulgar.'

He had never seen this side of her before. Granted, he hadn't known her all that long, nor even, if he were honest, all that well, but he would never have put her down as the avenging social angel type. She was clearly quite angry about something, though.

'Anyway,' she continued, the fire in her eyes dying down as suddenly as it had risen, 'I thought you would like the company.'

He blushed again and went back to his tax book.

'Are you really going to spend all of Christmas filling in your taxes, Richard?'

'I don't have a choice,' he replied, removing his glasses in what he hoped was a heroic fashion. 'I can't afford an accountant, and I just want them out of the way. You have to understand that you French are used to your bureaucracy, where as we foreigners find it absolutely terrifying. I'm sure you'd find half the Amazon rainforests just filed away in French departmental buildings somewhere. The paperwork is endless. I got stopped by the police the other day and I'd forgotten my papers. They made me go home and get them even though I knew them both and they knew me!'

She nodded, recognising the truth of what he'd said. 'You have either to shrug it off, or know how to handle the system,' she said. 'These people, they annoy me, the power they have. What did Balzac say? Bureaucracy is a giant mechanism operated by pigmies.' She started to pace the room again. He'd never heard her quote anything before, and it seemed to open a brief door to her. She shut it immediately. 'Why not give your accounts to my accountant? Then you could enjoy your Christmas!'

Something was up; he sensed it. She seemed strangely determined for him to enjoy the season of goodwill, which, despite being flattering, also felt out of character. Christmas, in Richard's eyes, was schmaltz and warm bonhomie; gaudy traditions, self-indulgence and hokey mush. It's why he loved it so much and could quote innumerable classic Hollywood Christmas lines just to let the whole sentimental slush wash over him. Valérie, though, was not the sentimental type. He also found it odd that she had an accountant. The more he learned about bounty hunters, the more mundane their world seemed to be. Though officially, of course, they were self-employed and therefore within the tentacles of the dreaded bureaucracy. He recalled the definition of 'Self-Employed' for the French authorities: 'a service provider working in an independent capacity and demonstrating specific qualifications sold to a third party'. Strange, he thought, how cold-eyed French pen-pushers made the thrilling world of the professional bounty hunter sound as dull as a door-to-door salesman peddling solar panels.

'That's very kind of you,' he said, 'but I really think I'm getting the hang of this now. It's not all that difficult when you...' He trailed off as Valérie picked up the large tax book and something else fell out. 'Ah,' he said meekly.

'What is this? What is the *Radio Times Christmas Bumper Edition*?' She opened a page at random. 'You have highlighted some things. Christmas Day, BBC2, 10.55am. *White Christmas*.'

'Well, yes...'

'Christmas Day, ITV2, 15.25, *The Great Escape*.'

'A classic,' he said, without making eye contact.

'Richard.' She didn't sound angry, it was more like compassion born of pity.

'Yes.' His reply was stoic.

'You were going to spend this Christmas alone watching old films?'

'Yes.' Now he was defiant.

'But you do not even have English television.'

'I was going to watch the DVDs. At the allotted time, according to the *Radio Times*.' He was aware that he now sounded somewhat deranged.

'Oh, Richard. How sad for you.'

He would leave it at that, he decided. Again, he was acutely aware that some people may indeed find the whole idea rather sad. Pitiable, in fact. He, however, had been looking forward to it immensely. *Christmas Eve*, he recalled, *Channel 4, 8.45pm. It's a Wonderful Life*.

'I think it's very lucky I came back,' she said, a sudden determination in her voice. 'To rescue you.' He knew that any other man in the world would swap places with him right now. A beautiful, exotic French lady of dubious profession was pinning him down for enjoyment.

He gulped and guiltily remembered: *28th December, BBC1, 2.45pm, Spartacus*.

'So,' she continued, 'what do you think of my idea? It will be fun, yes?'

Richard tried to remember how the conversation had started in the first place. Valérie had wafted in like a sudden warm breeze and started blathering excitedly about games and hunts and so on, and while he was absolutely delighted to see her, at the time he'd been wrestling with the difficult problem of how to watch both *The Wizard of Oz* and *The Return of the Pink Panther* when they overlapped by fifteen minutes.

'Yes, but what do you mean, fun?' He'd always felt the word to be a loaded one, to be held at arm's length like a rotting fish.

'What do you mean, what do you mean? Richard. Fun. It will be fun.' She didn't strike him as the kind to enjoy fun for fun's sake any more than he did, but she wasn't letting it go.

'I don't know,' he whined. 'I mean, these *games*…' He said the word 'games' like it was an illness. '…Scavenger hunts, murder mystery whodunnit stuff, fancy dress. These things take a lot of time to organise, you know? You can't just throw them together. Who's playing? Who's your victim? What's the motive? Are you looking for a murderer? There's so much to do to get these things right, and…' He opened his arms in a sympathetic gesture, but with the half-smile of a defending QC about to deliver a killing blow to the case for the prosecution. 'And, it's Christmas Eve tomorrow, we simply haven't got time now.'

He sat down again, pleased with himself, and re-opened the *Radio Times*. Valérie placed a card in front of him. She placed it like a poker player trumping someone else's hand:

By the terms of the will of
the late Sacha Bevellini,
your presence is required at a
Christmas Murder Hunt!
La Chasse Commence
Christmas Eve, 11am
Les Vignes Chambre d'hôte, Saint-Sauver

'These all went out last week, and everybody arrives tomorrow!'

Richard had rarely seen her so excited. He slouched back in his chair, defeated, head sunk into his chest.

'It's just a game.' She beamed.

He didn't believe a word of it.

Chapter Two

It was a scowling Richard that sat in the salon of his *chambre d'hôte* late the following morning. Of course, he had sensed that Valérie was up to something, although sensed might be overstating it as the woman was simply incapable of hiding her motives and, despite her profession, didn't seem inclined to subterfuge. He still felt like he'd been duped though and was thus determined to mope through the entire experience. Valérie was fussily setting up the drinks for the aperitif. There were ten champagne flutes, and he couldn't work out the maths behind that number. Allowing for a glass each for himself and Valérie, that left eight. The *chambre d'hôte* only had room for three couples, unless children had been invited too, which didn't seem likely for a murder mystery party. Not that he objected to children being around at Christmas; in his experience it stopped the adults behaving like children themselves.

'Why are there ten glasses?' he asked, trying hard not to sound interested.

9

She didn't look up as she laid out a selection of petits fours. 'There are four couples playing, and, of course, there are the two of us.'

'So I'm *not* playing?' Even he could hear the relief in his voice.

'In a way...' She looked at her watch. 'I haven't got time to explain now, people will be here soon.'

'So four couples?'

'Yes, Richard.'

'But where's the fourth couple staying?'

There was a knock at the door, and through the glass, Richard saw that the first of the couples had arrived. A tall, elegant woman entered without waiting for the door to be opened. She looked disapproving at first, then saw Valérie and broke into a well-practised media-type smile. The two women then did that Parisian women thing of air-kissing without touching and Richard felt like he was watching a wildlife documentary where two rival ostriches were about to fight to the death. 'Valérie,' said the taller woman without much warmth. 'It's been too long.'

'Ah!' Valérie held up her finger. 'We must maintain our aliases if the game is to work.'

'What fun,' the other woman replied, making it sound the exact opposite and therefore gaining Richard's sympathy.

'You are Comrade Rouge,' Valérie continued, ignoring the woman's tone entirely, 'and this is your husband, Monsieur le Maire Bleu!' A smaller, grey-haired man came through the door carrying a holdall, glasses steaming up as he entered the warmth of the salon.

'You didn't really think I'd be carrying your bags for you, did you—' he said petulantly, removing his battered beret.

'Your wife is called Comrade Rouge!' Valérie interrupted before he gave any identities away.

'Ha!' He snorted. 'Comrade indeed!'

'And the idea of you achieving the office of mayor is equally unlikely, wouldn't you say, *Monsieur* Bleu?' Comrade Rouge retorted. 'I mean, who would vote for you!'

Richard sat down. In his mind he saw a roaring log fire and on it, quickly aflame and soon turned to ashes, were the hopes of his quiet, non-family, non-warring Christmas. There was another knock at the door and even though it was open a gaunt man with a very pronounced Adam's apple peered in. His mouth was as wide open as the door, making him look like a baby bird who needed feeding.

'Is this, er…?'

'Of course it is, there's a sign on the gate!' He was bustled out of the way by a heavy-set woman whose shoulders were the widest part of her body, making her look practically square. One could almost have described her as having the physique of a formidable rugby player if it wasn't for the fact that she was also, improbably, wearing a ballgown, a heavy pearl necklace and a tiara.

'I am the Duchess Argentée,' she said grandly, 'and this is my chauffeur, Monsieur Vert.' She seemed to relish the introduction a little too much, which meant that one, she was keeping strictly to Valérie's assigned aliases and two, she regarded her husband as very much beneath her.

Further introductions were made between Comrade Rouge, Mayor Bleu, the Duchess Argentée and Monsieur Vert, and unless they were consummate actors, Richard had the impression that they didn't know each other. Though whether that meant anything at all, it was too early to say.

A tall young man now appeared in the doorway, his sharp eyes taking in everyone in the room. He smiled, though it came across as more of a sneer; the top lip slightly curved. His complexion was strangely ruddy too, which made him look like a young man with an old face, or an old man with a young face. Either way, to Richard there was something utterly dislikable about him and he reeked of ambition.

'Good afternoon,' he oiled, 'I believe I am Docteur Gris.'

Behind him stood an older woman, elegant and grey-haired. She had an air of authority, but also of exhausted dignity; like she needed to sit down for about a year.

'And I am Madame Noire.' She smiled, tired eyes taking in the room. 'I am the undertaker.' She then noticed the champagne glasses and perked up a little. 'Is one of those for me? I'm parched.'

Valérie handed out glasses to those who hadn't taken one – Mayor Bleu hadn't waited to be asked – and made more formal introductions. 'I'm very pleased,' she began, 'that you have all managed to come and that you have made such an effort with your outfits. Duchess Argentée, I must say that you look magnificent!'

'You are assuming, madame, that I do not dress like this anyway,' the woman huffed. 'I could easily do so if I wanted!'

'I do not doubt it,' Valérie said calmly before the woman could throw any more chip-on-the-shoulder resentment into the room.

'But who are *you*, madame?' It was Docteur Gris who asked the question and it wasn't couched with any great warmth. 'I presume that it was you who sent out the invitations. All very intriguing, obviously, and certainly it livens up what I find generally to be a dull time of year but,' his eyes narrowed, 'who are you?'

Richard could have told Docteur Gris that Valérie was not a woman to be hurried and harried and certainly not intimidated, and what was clearly meant, on his part, to be a domineering sneer should be abandoned quickly. Valérie's eyes turned cold as she met his look. Briefly, he tried to fight back, but it was a futile gesture and instead he broke into a smile that suggested he'd been joking all along. Richard noticed his partner's face; it hadn't changed much, but there was a twinkle in the eye that suggested the 'undertaker', Madame Noire, had enjoyed his defeat immensely.

'We are still waiting for another couple to arrive, so I will save the explanations until then. There is no sense in repeating everything. Until then, and I hope they won't be long,' Valérie looked at Richard as if he were somehow responsible, 'let us enjoy this champagne.

13

Remember, though, it is vital for the game that you maintain your aliases.'

'Who are the other couple?' Richard asked as Valérie handed him a long-overdue glass of champagne.

Valérie was looking at her watch. 'Martin and Gennie Thompson,' she replied distractedly.

'Oh no! Really?' It wasn't that Richard disliked Martin and Gennie Thompson, but that they brought baggage. They lived in the next town, were English, like Richard, and ran a *chambre d'hôte*, also like Richard. That, as he repeated to Valérie whenever the opportunity arose, was where the similarities ended. Their sideline, if something as in your face as a swingers society could be a sideline, was running a more specialist establishment catering for anything from minor, bizarre peccadilloes to more extreme, in Richard's opinion, perversions. To look at them though, with their matching raincoats and butter-wouldn't-melt expressions, you wouldn't know it. However, it turned out that Gennie was a volcano of barely suppressed passion while Martin, if making double entendres out of nothing were an Olympic sport, would be Usain Bolt. Richard was at least thankful that with it being winter, their penchant for naturism wouldn't rear its ugly head. In short, Richard found them hard work. 'Why Martin and Gennie, though?'

'Because, Richard, they are good at breaking the ice, where you are more…' She paused, searching for the right word, 'controlled. Yes, you are more controlled. They have a way of lowering people's guards.'

14

Richard wondered what Martin's double entendre talent would have made of that last sentence, and may have even tried it himself too if it wasn't for the slur on his character as a chatty host.

'Pfft!' he snorted. 'I didn't realise it was going to be *that* kind of game!'

'I thought that the English liked Christmas parlour games,' she replied, missing his point entirely.

'No, we like massive over-indulgence, falling asleep, and sandwiches on Boxing Day. The fact that the French don't even *have* a Boxing Day is a massive discredit to what otherwise is a great nation.' He downed his champagne in triumph.

'Can I top you up, monsieur?' It was the mayor, Monsieur Bleu, with a smile slightly chillier than the bottle he was holding.

'Thank you,' Richard said, beaming as he did so, trying not to be 'controlled', as Valérie put it.

'And are you to take part in this game, monsieur?'

Richard looked at Valérie and, for the first time, realised that he had absolutely no idea of his role in all this, other than as an apparently menacing presence and truculent host.

Valérie stepped in quickly. 'This,' she said, raising her voice to get everyone's attention, 'is Papa Noël.'

It was the kind of statement that got people's attention, especially as Papa Noël was currently wearing a crimson cardigan and brown corduroy trousers, sipping from a champagne glass.

'Shouldn't he be getting ready?' smirked Docteur Gris.

'Why am I Papa Noël?' Richard hissed.

'Because I prefer *Papa* to *Père*,' she said, matter of factly. 'I adore the song "Petit Papa Noël". Do you know it? It's by Tino Rossi.'

Ignoring what a well-qualified psychiatrist would make of the distinction between *père* and *papa*, Richard realised that she had, as usual, completely missed his point.

'I adore that Christmas carol also,' said the already slightly worse for wear undertaker, Madame Noire, propped up in the corner. And then she began to sing it. It was oddly melancholic the way she did so before everyone else in the room joined in the impromptu concert and even Richard, who resented what he regarded as his purely ceremonial role in the upcoming affair, couldn't fail to be moved by it. When they had finished, there was a brief embarrassed silence and then they all laughed nervously.

'I think,' said Valérie, 'that we should start. The other team to arrive will be with Papa Noël. I can explain the rules to them later.'

'Are you English, monsieur?' It was the Duchess Argentée who asked.

'I am,' he replied, 'though I like to think that Papa Noël is a citizen of the world,' he added grandly.

'How do we know that he won't cheat?' Docteur Gris asked.

'Because I am English,' Richard replied, standing straight-backed as though he were Phileas Fogg. He wasn't usually in the least affronted by such comments, but he'd taken a dislike to the man.

'That, monsieur, is no longer a guarantee of probity,' Comrade Rouge said caustically, though with a raised and slightly flirtatious eyebrow.

'Bloody cheek!' Richard replied. 'Well you won't get any presents!'

'Rich— sorry, Papa Noël is above any suspicion. I can vouch for him and he will work with our fourth couple.'

'You are not a couple?' Monsieur Vert asked, speaking for the first time. There was a brief look of hope in his eyes as if not being a couple was a lofty personal ambition; the promised land. He was immediately admonished by the duchess for speaking at all.

'Don't mind him,' she said in a terribly posh, terribly false accent. 'I could have done so much better,' she smiled, half-joking. 'I call him my tattoo, don't I, dear?' She chuckled. 'I mean that he was a wine-fuelled fancy and now I can't get rid of him.'

'I married the wrong sister,' Monsieur Vert said with hollow humour, then quietly added, 'God rest her soul.'

The duchess ignored him and asked what for her was clearly the more pressing question: 'What do we inherit anyway?' She tried to make it sound as if she didn't really care. 'The invitation says it's a will, a legacy. What does that mean, exactly? I don't think we're related. I did some research online, I'd never heard of this regular Christmas thing before…'

'Nor I,' Doctor Gris added as if that were the last word on the matter. It wasn't.

'And it seems,' the duchess continued, throwing an annoyed look at her interrupter, 'that in previous years the winners of this game mustn't reveal anything about themselves or what they won.'

'Yes, why is it all so secretive?' It was unclear if Doctor Gris meant to snarl, but that's certainly how it came across. What was clear to Richard though, was that despite not knowing what they were going to inherit, if that was the right word, this odd group of mostly unpleasant people had come anyway. It was like being surrounded by six Veruca Salts.

'This video will explain everything,' Valérie said calmly, opening her laptop. Everyone gathered in closely around Richard's breakfast bar as she pressed a button and the screen lit up. She pressed Play.

A silhouette slowly appeared, but it was difficult to tell whether it was a man or a woman. If it was the mysterious philanthropist Sacha Bevellini, then the name gave nothing away either. The body was heavy-set, and what light there was just touched the blue-grey of their hair. In the background was an austere-looking bookcase giving the impression of seriousness; that this was an official declaration, in fact. The person on screen began talking, while remaining in the shadows, but the voice had been deliberately slowed down, so there was still no idea of the gender.

Merry Christmas, the character started with a chuckle. *I assume the world still exists at Christmas and that you have kindly accepted my invitation. I have been dead for some years, yet here I am, right now, alive and with you. Ah, the wonders of the world, my friends!*

I miss life! You are fortunate you still have that precious commodity, that gift that only God can give – life must be cherished, it must be lived to the full, it must be enjoyed! I am giving you that chance. This game that I set forth every year, it is my humble gift. I am not trying to be God in any way, but I learned a great thing: Money can *buy you happiness, it* can *buy you a life. If you complete the tasks that are set before you, you will each inherit happiness, that power of vivacity, and the richness that that reward brings. I make one stipulation of the teams that my lawyers assemble, and they have assembled you discreetly. The teams must meet two criteria: they must have social or political influence and they must also, forgive me, be impecunious. It is not as rare a combination as you might think; those with influence often live beyond their means, but you, my friends, know that full well, do you not?*

There was an awkward silence and avoiding of each others' eyes following this statement, but no argument either. The shadowy figure chuckled again and clapped their hands like an excited child. Richard caught Valérie's eye in the meantime and made it perfectly clear that if this was indeed Sacha Bevellini, then they were a few needles short of a full Christmas tree, so to speak. She shrugged in response.

So the task before you is a simple one, and this is the game. Who am I? And who murdered me?

There were some excited murmurs among the watching couples.

One last thing, enjoy yourselves! It's Christmas, and it could be your best yet! Oh, I do wish that I could be with you, to see your faces when you solve the mystery, but I leave you in capable hands — and who knows? I may even reappear to offer clues, clues from your talking corpse…

This was followed by another chuckle, which broke into a severe coughing fit. The room fell into silence again, and felt oddly cold too as the screen faded. 'Well, that's as clear as mud,' slurred Madame Noire, whose comment was ignored as everyone carried on staring at the now-blank screen.

Suddenly the door flew open, causing the duchess to scream, spooked as she was by the video message, and in fell Martin and Gennie dressed as elves, but the most inappropriate elves it was possible to be without actually being in a top-shelf magazine.

'Have we missed anything?' Martin breathed heavily.

'You see?' Valérie said to Richard. 'They break the ice!'

Chapter Three

Martin and Gennie's dramatic entrance certainly punctured what had become a tense atmosphere. It was clear that following the short video explanation, each couple – Martin and Gennie aside – were already in competition mode and trying to work out an early strategy. One of the rules that had been laid down was that there should be no collusion between the teams. Richard didn't see that as a problem at all; they all seemed to loathe each other, as well as their partners. It was interesting to note that none of them contested what had been said about them. That they were people of influence could be inferred largely by their manner, they weren't going to argue about that, but that they were all on their uppers too, that was less obvious. Though it seemed that that's exactly what they were. Richard tutted loudly and involuntarily; he was probably going to be expected to serve free food too.

They slowly drifted off to their allotted rooms, leaving Richard, Valérie and two middle-aged erotic elves in the salon. Valérie had replayed the video to

Martin and Gennie and then she had explained that they were, with Richard, to act as her eyes and ears 'on the ground', so to speak. There had then been a brief silence as they weighed things up, a silence broken only by the squeaking of the elves' PVC outfits, and Richard had tried to concentrate on anything but Martin and Gennie, who, if he'd been asked, were the least erotic thing he had seen in some considerable time.

'Won't you be too cold dressed like that?' Valérie asked, for once concentrating on practicalities.

It was Martin who replied first. 'Oh, I'm glad you said that Val, I'm certainly getting a draught.' He pulled up his tights as if that would help the situation.

'Me too,' Gennie agreed, though thankfully didn't make any flamboyant costume adjustments.

'But what's all this really about, Val, anyway?' Martin asked, his fidgeting finally stopping.

'Yes, I was going to ask that,' Gennie broke in. 'I mean, it looks fun and all that, even if Mr Scrooge over there hasn't got a costume.'

Richard managed to feel both resentful and pleased at the comment.

'Oh, it is just a game!' Valérie beamed.

'I didn't know you were into games,' Martin said, unable to help himself while Gennie gave him a nudge, though she chuckled at the same time and Richard rolled his eyes.

'I was in Paris and I was bored,' Valérie began, 'and I thought that I would come to Saint-Sauver for Christmas, but what to do? Eat and drink, drink and eat…' She looked at Richard, who thought that that had the makings of a great plan. 'So I read about these so-called murder games, dinner party hunts, and I thought that would be fun.'

Thirty minutes later, Richard and Valérie were driving into town alone. Martin and Gennie, their roles having been explained, had gone home to add warmth to their costumes, leaving the other two to make preparations.

'So it's not real, then?' Richard asked. 'It is just a game.'

'What do you feel?' Valérie replied enigmatically while changing gear on her throaty sports car.

'Well, if it is just a game, I think you're going to have some very disappointed players. Some of them, maybe not all, believe it, and they smell riches.'

'Riches?'

'Yes, riches. Dead millionaires, legacies, wealth.'

'Oh, do you think so?' was her innocent reply.

'You know so. These people are short of money, and they think they're going to win some. According to the duchess, even Wikipedia says they'll win some.'

Valérie parked the car outside the *boulangerie* and turned the engine off. She seemed pensive, as though trying to make her mind up about something, but in the end, she said nothing. It was perfectly obvious to Richard that something was going on, and that the exasperating woman was trying to decide just how much she should tell him. He thought about staying in the car and sulking, but decided against it and joined her in the queue stretching outside the busy *boulangerie*. The decorations hanging across the street glistened in the winter sunshine, and as people spoke and exchanged festive greetings, their breath hung in the air like misty clouds. It was hard, even for Richard, who had had his traditional seasonal plans scuppered, not to feel Christmassy; a feeling he enjoyed immensely, even if he was currently missing *In Which We Serve* on BBC2.

'So you're not going to tell me what's really going on then?' he said, trying to keep it light as he joined Valérie in the queue.

She looked up at him and sighed, causing his spectacles to cloud over as a result. She smiled apologetically and removed his glasses, allowing them to hang on their string.

'That makes you look older you know, that string. You do not have an old face.'

He smiled. 'Madame d'Orçay, I do believe that you are changing the subject.'

She nodded. 'OK.' She sighed heavily again as though what she was about to say was being done so under duress. 'I am trying to do two jobs with the one stone.'

'You mean kill two birds with one stone?' he said, trying to be helpful.

'What are you talking about?' was her irritated response.

'Never mind, slightly different idioms. What jobs?'

They shuffled forward in the queue as Richard acknowledged an acquaintance emerging from the *fromagerie* across the road. 'I told you that I was in Paris, and I did not like it. Passepartout did not like it either. He was very restless.'

'So he fancied some time in the country, did he?'

'Don't mock me, Richard, please. I am trying to explain.'

'Right-o.' He hadn't meant to mock her at all, but she was obviously taking this very seriously.

'I have been asked to do a job. The job is almost what you saw on the video. Dead and wealthy client wants others to enjoy life.'

'Almost?'

'Almost, yes.'

'And is your client a man or a woman?'

'There is such a thing as client confidentiality, Richard.'

'Even if the client is dead?'

'Well, I have a duty to the estate, obviously!'

They shuffled forward again, this time making it through the door and into the warmth of the *boulangerie*. Jeanine, the *boulangère*, had gone all out on Christmas decorations and, together with the smell, it added to the festive season even more. Jeanine herself, a long-time admirer of Richard's who, she was convinced, looked like the Earl of Grantham in *Downton Abbey*, wore a Father Christmas hat and had a bunch of mistletoe pinned to the front. On seeing Richard and Valérie, she came bustling around the counter and looked up at the much-taller Richard.

'I watched the Christmas episode of *Downton Abbey* last night, Richard. Now I know the English tradition of kissing under the mistletoe!' She stood on her tip-toes, and Richard awkwardly bent down and kissed her cheek, which he would do anyway if he met her in

25

the street, both cheeks in fact, but the mistletoe added an extra frisson. Valérie gave their order and reserved various breads and *bûches* for the following day.

'Jeanine,' Valérie asked, 'was my package delivered?'

For a moment, Jeanine looked blank and then rolled her eyes. 'Oh, of course! Silly me. I forget sometimes that I am now an Amazon drop-off point. It's not really caught on here yet, but it will, I suppose.' She disappeared into the back of the shop and came back with a flat, square box which she handed to Valérie. Richard thought he saw a wink between the two, but he was probably imagining it.

'So,' he said, as Valérie restarted the engine and pulled off. 'You have an assignment to complete and managed to turn it into a game so you could move it out of Paris. That way, you could persuade those involved to follow you here.'

He didn't look at her as he said this, but he was very aware that she had, as usual, taken her eyes off the road and was looking at him. 'You are very clever, Richard. Yes. Also, forgive me, I knew you would be on your own, you told me so, and I need your help.'

'Somewhere to put everyone up, you mean?' he asked, trying not to sound disappointed at the prosaic nature of his role.

'More than that, Richard. I *really* need your help. I cannot do this alone. It's a game. Now I don't think you like games any more than I do, but you know more about them, I feel. You will have seen them in films, how they work. I need your expertise.'

It all sounded very thin to Richard. Yes, of course, he could reel off any number of films based around murder hunts, scavenger hunts, odd legacies of wills, all of that.

'Also,' Valérie continued, a jaunty, enthusiastic tone coming into her voice, 'my client really is dead. And one of those people, I think, really is the murderer.'

She smiled broadly at him, and now he was even less sure whether it was a game or not. 'Is that the truth?' he asked, letting out a long, deep sigh.

Valérie tried not to sound hurt by his doubt. 'Of course, Richard!'

'Because you really do have a way of telling the truth that sounds like you're lying,' he said after a pause. 'But I can always tell when you are lying, because you're rubbish at it.'

'So?' She smiled again, and he laughed.

'So? So I have no idea what's going on now!'

'Anyway,' she nodded over her shoulder to Passepartout on the backseat. 'We don't like Christmas alone.' She shrugged as if that were an end to the matter, which, as far as Richard was concerned, it was. He was none the wiser. Either he was in a game, or he had a real-life murderer staying in his posh B&B. One thing he did know about Valérie was that you just had to hold on tight and try to enjoy the ride.

'What's in the package, anyway?' he asked after a few more moments of silence.

'Ah,' Valérie enthused, 'your present.' Richard panicked immediately. He hadn't been expecting her to stay, so

27

he hadn't bought her anything in return. Typical, he thought, wondering what at this late stage would be available in the supermarket.

Valérie breathed in heavily and it sounded like disappointment, as though she knew he hadn't got her anything.

'Do you need any last-minute things from the super-market?' To Richard she sounded wounded. 'I want to drop some clothes off for charity anyway.'

'Er, yes,' he replied, trying to sound nonchalant. 'We need some lemons.'

She gave him an odd look as she turned into the supermarket car park before stopping carefully next to the large, white charity clothes bins where a pile of clothes had been dumped at the base and near the already overflowing bottle banks. Richard briefly wondered if the Follet Valley was ready for such largesse, whether the poor and needy of the area could cope with cast-off Parisian haute couture. He doubted it, he doubted it very much.

'Richard,' Valérie said, 'could you put this bag of clothing in the collection bin for me, please? It's quite heavy.'

Muttering to himself, he got out and grabbed a large bin-liner from the backseat. It weighed a tonne. 'What on earth have you put in here?' he asked, struggling so that the bag wouldn't split.

'A few old coats, some boots, trousers and so on.'

He made it the few yards to the clothes bin and, with Valérie standing behind him, gave a heave to lift the bag into the revolving tray. Just as he did so the bag split and an assortment of the chicest fashions fell down onto a heap of previously dumped much-dirtier, older and far-less-glamorous apparel lying on the floor. 'Bloody hell!' he griped, and bent down to gather up the two piles of clothing.

'Ow!' something in the heap said. 'What do you want to go and do that for?' Richard leapt back as the dirtier clothes on the bottom began to form a human shape, and the dirty face of an old woman glowered at him from between Valérie's cast-off skirts.

'I'm terribly sorry!' he stammered and looked at Valérie for support, who didn't offer any.

'You're supposed to put that stuff in the bin, not on sleeping old women!' the woman in the clothes pile reprimanded Richard.

'I'm sorry!' he said again.

'Well, anyway. I'm awake now, aren't I?' She smacked her lips together. 'Got any booze?'

'Who are you?' Valérie asked quietly.

'What does it matter? I'm no one. No one.'

'You must have a name, though?'

'And what's it to you?' Valérie shrugged and pretended to be uninterested. 'It's Blanche,' the woman said quickly. 'Blanche Noel.'

'White Christmas?' Richard's jaw dropped.

'No! Not bloody White Christmas. Blanche Noel. Nole.' She pronounced it clearly. 'Not No-El.'

Richard had decided she was White Christmas anyway, he was having no truck with missing umlauts.

'And where are you sleeping tonight, madame?' Valérie asked, and Richard remembered her words on the homeless of Paris earlier that day.

'Here,' was the reply. 'Or there.' She pointed at the adjoining bin.

'But it will be minus three tonight!' Valérie seemed frantic.

'Ah. I've got everything I need. Except booze. Are you sure you haven't got any booze?'

'Yes, we have,' Valérie said quickly, 'back at home. Lots of it. You must come with us!' Valérie heaved the woman and her bags and rags into the back of her car, causing Passepartout to sniff the air with a grimace.

Richard was left staring at the white charity clothes bins, his back to the car, and wondering if he could get away with a 'No Room at the Inn' speech on Christmas Eve. He knew that he could not, and he also knew it would be futile to try. He got into the car silently and wondered what it must be like to have some control over your life. His day had started off with the *Radio Times* and a highlighter. It now had a murder hunt, erotic goblins, bickering couples and a boozed-up tramp. It was going to be a long Christmas.

Chapter Four

By mid-afternoon, everybody had reconvened in Richard's salon, all in various moods which ran the full spectrum from excitement, through apprehension and to the further extreme of thunderously grouchy, which was just Richard. He had been perfectly willing to accept Valérie's vague, potentially contradictory explanation of what was going on. He had resigned himself to the ride. He had also, though he had eventually put up a struggle when he lost his bedroom, accepted that it was a charitable and seasonal thing to do to offer shelter to a tramp for Christmas. But he had not been prepared for his 'present', which turned out to be his game costume. And worse, he had forgotten to get a present for Valérie and they were still low on lemons.

He now sat brooding in the corner of the salon dressed as Papa Noël, a bulging sack sewn onto his padded red onesie, and a look on his face that had very little to do with the season of goodwill and which even his elasticated white beard couldn't hide. And it wasn't just the costume, it was the size of it. It was, at a very conservative estimate, at least three sizes too small; he looked like he'd been shrink-wrapped. So right now, he couldn't care less for games, freezing drunk tramps or potential murderers, nor even for the femme fatale nature of Valérie, which he had fallen for once again. No, right now, he felt like barricading himself in his cinema room, which was now doubling as his bedroom anyway, and overdosing on pure, industrial-strength bah humbug.

He had assumed, wrongly, that his role of referee, observer, call it what you will, would have an element of dignity about it. He imagined William Powell in *My Man Godfrey*, plucked from the streets by the beautiful Carole Lombard in a madcap and romantic scavenger hunt. But no, this wasn't Hollywood in 1936, this was Valérie's world in twenty-first-century rural France, and he felt and looked like a berk.

'Champagne, Monsieur Noël?' Docteur Gris toyed with his pretend stethoscope as he looked down at him, a smirk on his face so poisonous it would have got him struck off in any civilised society. 'Or are you driving a sleigh later?'

Valérie strode to the centre of the room and clapped her hands to get everyone's attention. She was the only one not in a character costume, choosing for herself something equally arresting but more along the lines of Honor Blackman in *Goldfinger*. A smart, fitted business suit, high-heeled boots and a heavy woollen scarf.

'*Mesdames et messieurs,*' she said in a loud voice, 'I think it is time we began.'

The people in the room who were talking to each other, which wasn't many of them, stopped. Martin and Gennie, who were now wearing more demure outfits with just green hats to indicate their elviness, topped people's glasses up one last time.

Valérie broke the wax seal on a large brown envelope and removed some documents. 'So,' she began, 'we have four teams. Our three couples, Duchesse Argentée and Monsieur Vert, Madame Noire and Docteur Gris, Comrade Rouge and le Maire Bleu. We also have Papa Noël,' Richard grunted, 'and his *lutins*.' Martin and Gennie both chuckled. 'The objective of the game is to find out the identity of the "victim", your benefactor.'

'Victim?' It was Madame Noire who asked the question.

'For the purposes of the game, madame, and according to these instructions, we need a victim. The clues that I will give you, per instruction, will lead to other clues. Those clues will reveal not only the victim's identity but how that person died. Are there any questions so far?'

'So we are looking for a murderer?' Comrade Rouge made it sound run-of-the-mill, a chore.

'You must decide that for yourselves Comrade Rouge. Follow the clues which will lead you on a path around this area. Once you have the victim and the cause of death, you must decide if it was the result of foul play. It is for you to decide.'

There was some murmuring among the group, and Valérie raised her voice again. 'I have four envelopes here, one for each team. The clues in each envelope are identical, so I will release you at ten-minute intervals. Is that clear?'

Again there was murmuring assent from most of the group. Only the duchess seemed compelled to question the game. 'It doesn't seem very dignified, does it?' she said, nose slightly in the air. 'Chasing around the countryside like this?'

'But Madame la Duchesse,' it was Madame Noire, 'think of the money!' She snorted in derision and took another gulp of the champagne.

'But we don't even know how much that is, do we?' the duchess continued.

'Can you not give us a hint?' her chauffeur husband Monsieur Vert asked Valérie.

'Don't be so vulgar!' his wife snapped at him. He had had the nerve to articulate her own greed, and she was almost puce with anger. 'Anyway, we may as well get on with it, I suppose.'

Valérie gave the couple an envelope and said they could go. She timed the ten-minute intervals like an official at a sports event, running everything by the book. All the teams took their envelopes and left slowly, pretending not to be competitive, all except Comrade Rouge and Mayor Bleu who positively raced to their car.

Richard had remained seated during all of this and stayed so now. He had no burning desire to go running around his adopted home town dressed as a mockery of Father Christmas, especially if he was in competition with a murderer. The whole thing seemed somewhat fraught with dangerous possibilities, and he was perfectly prepared to down his sack, stamp his boots and not play.

He stood up slowly. 'I'll go and feed my hens before we set off,' he said, making it sound more like he was about to go to his office and take the gentleman's way out.

He trudged off and spent the next five minutes complaining loudly to his remaining hens, Lana Turner and Joan Crawford. Ava Gardner having been the victim of a mafia assassination, her space in the coop was still conspicuous. The two hens offered what support they could, and Richard, as always feeling a touch brighter for the experience, returned to the salon and his fate.

He did not expect to encounter his doppelgänger as he did so.

There, in earnest conversation with Valérie and his teammates Martin and Gennie, was Father Christmas. He wore the same padded suit, the same pathetic sack sewn onto his shoulder and, Richard couldn't help noticing, the same look of embarrassed resignation that was under his own false beard but, and this was crucial, the outfit fitted like a glove.

'Now what's going on?' he bleated. 'Have you kidnapped a local child?'

'Ah,' Valérie replied, 'there is a little twist.'

The second Papa Noël lowered his beard and gave Richard a put-upon smile. 'Bonjour, Monsieur Ainsworth,' he said stiffly.

'Monsieur Mabit!' Richard cried. 'So she's roped you in too, eh?' Monsieur Mabit was the town fixer, a ceremonial bureaucrat who basically ran the place, though no one could remember where he came from nor how he got into such positions of civic power. In fact, if asked to describe the diminutive Mabit at all, most people would fail to do so. The man had an almost permanent anonymity, but he was a fellow victim of Valérie's powers of persuasion.

'Now,' Valérie interrupted, 'you three must go.' She was addressing Martin, Gennie and Mabit now hiding once again behind his beard. She gave an envelope to Gennie. 'I will see you this evening.' They left hurriedly, leaving Richard and Valérie alone in the salon. Richard slumped down in his chair again.

'No, Richard, there is no time for you to sit down.'

He stood up immediately. 'What,' he asked, 'is going on now?'

She looked at her watch. 'There is not much time to explain.' She looked over both shoulders as if she might be overheard.

'Is someone else hiding in the dresser?' he asked sceptically. 'I assume that's where Mabit was hiding. He didn't hang around, did he? Straight into my role—'

'This is no time for jealousy, Richard. Monsieur Mabit will do as he's told.' It was an odd reply, partly because if obedience was what Valérie was demanding, then Richard couldn't ever remember rebelling against her. 'Now look, I want you to stay here. It's possible that one of them might come back, maybe try to find out

36

the identities of the other players. Also, you must keep an eye on Blanche, I think she may be an alcoholic...'

'You don't say?'

'And, most importantly, Richard...' She gave him a deadly serious look, suggesting the fine line between life and death, though also showing a touch of vulnerability, so he made sure she knew he was taking this seriously.

'Yes, what is it?'

She held up a diamanté dog lead. 'Please look after Passepartout. This could be dangerous.'

So that was it. He'd gone from major player Papa Noël, albeit in a children's costume, to keeper of the drinks cabinet and dog walker and still in a children's costume. He wondered if it was too late to ask the real Father Christmas for the gift of dignity.

'Right,' he said tetchily, snatching the lead. 'I'll do my best.'

'Oh and, Richard?' She turned as she reached the door.

'Yes, what now? Is there some ironing you want doing?'

'You can be a very silly man,' she said dismissively. 'There was an extra envelope, can you take it for me? I must go. I will see you later.'

She left the envelope on the side by the coffee, gave Passepartout a dramatic parting hug, and left.

Half an hour later, Richard was in his cinema room. He had bought two rows of four fold-down cinema seats at a local *brocante* some years before, and he sat at the front on the end, his favourite place. Passepartout was in his throne, wedged into a seat on the other end, looking like he was in a sinking ship. To placate himself, Richard had deferred his planned viewing of Hitchcock's *Suspicion* and gone instead with something more relevant, *The Last of Sheila*. There was something about late-period James Mason and his careworn insouciance that suited Richard's mood, but as it was also a film about a murder hunt it helped him feel more involved.

The only thing ruining the atmosphere was Blanche snoring loudly on the seats behind him, cradling a bottle of cooking rum she had found in the kitchen.

He still had the envelope Valérie had given him, and he turned it over in his hand. So far, he had resisted the temptation to open it, but his self-discipline was beginning to crack. There was something heavier than just paper in the envelope too, and it was eating away at him. Finally, making sure Blanche was still asleep and ignoring Passepartout's jaundiced eye, he succumbed to the temptation and carefully opened the flap. Inside was a small silver Yale-type key, too small for a door he felt, but also too big for a padlock too. There was a note with it.

*Aujourd'hui est le jour pour
vous livrer des livres.*

It didn't really make any sense. 'Today is the day to deliver yourself of books,' he said to himself. 'Or, today is the day you give yourself up if the verb "livrer" is reflexive? Or, *livres* could mean pounds sterling.' He tapped the key on the palm of his left hand, thinking and examining it again. Its ridges were sharp, suggesting it had been recently cut, and the conclusion gave him confidence. It also had the number 24 stamped on it. He kept tapping away. Humphrey Bogart would know immediately what to do. He'd have tapped the key into the palm of his hand too, then snapped his fingers, pointed at an assistant and run out of the door heading for the train station, because train stations have lockers and people hid things in lockers and he'd have started with locker 24. Richard wasn't even sure that train stations still had lockers, certainly not Saint-Sauver, which rarely even had trains. He felt compelled to try anyway though, just like his hero. Bogart, however, wouldn't have been dog-sitting, nor would he have been watching a film either, especially one in which the organiser of the murder hunt is horribly killed halfway through. *That could be Valérie*, Richard thought suddenly. *If this was like The Last of Sheila, she might be in danger.*

He stood up. 'Well,' he said valiantly, 'if in doubt, follow the Bogart.'

'Down in front!' slurred Blanche and fell off her seat.

Chapter Five

Of course, though grateful that Valérie had ditched the idea of him chasing about as Papa Noël, despite this meaning he was demoted to a supporting role, it did leave him in a quandary. He would have to adopt some form of disguise at least, or he'd be recognised. And despite not being entirely sure why he shouldn't be recognised, he felt he ought to make an effort nonetheless. He found an old beret and a blue overall, the uniform of the agricultural Frenchman and wrapped one of Valérie's less-flamboyant scarves around the bottom half of his chin, which meant that he now looked like a Parisian trying to look like an agricultural Frenchman, but it would have to do. Then he realised that he couldn't take his car either.

His beloved and battered old 2CV, which Clare had once described as being symbolic of their marriage in that 'it's a surprise it's still going', had LES VIGNES – CHAMBRE D'HÔTE advertised on the doors and was therefore hardly conducive to keeping a low profile. There was nothing else for it. Clare's bike. It was no less battered than Richard's 2CV, but at least the basket on the front would come in handy. It squeaked as he wheeled it out of the shed. Richard had bought it for Clare a few Christmasses ago. It was a romantic and clearly blinding error. 'So, you think I need exercise, do you?' she'd demanded, 'I need to lose weight, is that it?'

'I'll show her,' he said under his breath. 'I'll show them both,' he said to a bemused Passepartout as he placed him in the basket, wrapping the bony thing in a blanket like ET, before setting off on the road. Twenty-five minutes later, a sweaty-looking Parisian dressed as an agricultural *paysan* was hyperventilating in the centre of Saint-Sauver. Richard stopped and sat on a bench opposite the café-bar. The train station was still another three kilometres away, up a slight incline too, so he decided to re-read the clue and also to talk himself out of going to the station and its left-luggage lockers, at least for now. Then he noticed, sitting at an outside table smoking a cigarette with a glass of wine in front of her, was Madame Noire. Standing beside her was Docteur Gris. From where he sat, Richard couldn't hear what was being said, but it was clear that the so-called docteur was remonstrating with his partner and, judging by the coolness of her posture, basically telling her that she wasn't pulling her weight. The younger man threw his arms up in frustration and stormed off towards the post office. *Of course!* thought Richard, *the post office! They have lockers too! As does Jeanine with her Amazon deliveries.* A wave of relief came over him as he realised he didn't need to cycle all the way out to the station.

The trick though was to get to either the post or the *boulangerie* without being seen. He was quite pleased with his disguise, but he'd rather not run too much of a risk. From his bench, he could see the front door of the post office and watched as Docteur Gris walked in. Richard decided to get back on his bike and cycle around to Jeanine's bakery instead; it had taken him a long time to get there, but he might get ahead of the others as only Martin, Gennie and Mabit knew that Jeanine was now taking parcel deliveries. Also, Richard was relieved to remember, she sold cold drinks.

'Jeanine!' he called from the back door of the *boulangerie*. Two younger men in white overalls and hygiene hairnets were preparing a fresh batch of dough. They looked at him and ignored him. 'Jeanine!' he called again, and this time one of the bakers went to get his *patronne*. 'Ah, madame,' Richard said, making his French accent as strong as possible and pulling the scarf higher up his face. He squinted his eyes too, having pulled the beret lower.

'Richard! What are you doing?'

He pulled his scarf down in irritation. 'How did you know it was me?'

She looked at him oddly. 'Why shouldn't it be you? It looks like you.'

'Never mind. Look, I know this sounds odd, but can I have a look at your Amazon lockers?' He was glad Martin wasn't there to make something out of that.

'You too?' She gave him a reproving look which didn't last long. 'Martin, Gennie and Père Noël were here not long ago asking exactly the same. I can't do that, they're private property.'

'Dammit,' he said, and thought about his options. 'Have you got a bottle of water?'

She bustled off and returned quickly. 'What's this all about, anyway?' she asked, handing him the cold bottle.

'Oh, it's just a game, a murder hunt. Valérie's idea. It's a lot of fun,' he added unconvincingly.

She looked dubious. 'Are you sure she's right for you?'

'Right for me?' he replied quickly. 'Oh, we're not together!'

'Oh!' There was now a look of hope in her eyes. 'Well, she must have some pull on you, you're hot and sweaty, in disguise, and asking to break into private property!'

He took the key out of his pocket. Jeanine was right; what on earth was he doing? Going off half-cocked on some vague wild goose chase, no idea what was behind it other than one of the others might, *might*, be a murderer.

'Is that the key you want to try in my lockers?' she asked him gently, a tinge of sympathy in her voice.

'Yes, yes it is.' He gave her a closer look at it.

'Well, it's not the right one. It's too big.'

'Oh. Oh well.' He put it back in his pocket, deflated.

'That's more your cupboard-sized key, that.'

Suddenly his eyes flashed and he had an idea. 'Oh, Jeanine, you're wonderful!' He kissed her on both cheeks and jumped back on his bicycle. '*Bonnes fêtes!*' he shouted as he pedalled off, with the clue reverberating round his head, '*Aujourd'hui est le jour pour vous livrer des livres.*'

He didn't know why it hadn't occurred to him before, and he wondered if he should have asked Jeanine if she'd given the same information to any of the others. It didn't sound like she had, but he had to be careful all the same, and he decided to take the back streets of Saint-Sauver on his return to the market square. The route took him past the library, which made him doubt his solution, so he slowed down to re-gather his thoughts. The large glass front of the library was awash with light, with Christmas decorations and children's drawings on the windows; it looked warm and inviting. He got off his bike and thought he might as well check it out while he was here. After all, the clue, if he'd read the thing right, did talk about books, but where did the key element fit in? Do libraries have lockers? They certainly have cupboards.

He propped his bicycle up by a lamp-post, careful not to wake the sleeping chihuahua, bowed his head and crossed the road. He was about to go in through the big double doors when he noticed that the duchess and her put-upon husband were in there already. They were at the counter and Monsieur Vert was holding up their key, asking questions of the polite but confused-looking librarian, questions prompted by his harrying wife. The librarian said something, looking apologetic. Monsieur Vert looked grateful but disappointed in response, while the duchess had a look on her face like she'd been chewing on cloves and stormed towards the door. Richard turned away immediately, jumped back on his bike and went with his original idea.

The market square of Saint-Sauver was largely empty. It only housed the market once a week on a Thursday morning, so the rest of the time, it was used as a car park. There was a large Christmas tree in the middle that threw out a warm light, and the plane trees that lined the square on three sides also had lights hanging from them. It was a perfect Christmas card image, but Richard had his mind on other things. He hid behind one of the larger plane trees directly across the square from his objective. The *boîte à livres*.

As far as Richard was aware, this kind of small, municipal book exchange was happening all over the place. In the UK, he'd heard that old telephone boxes were being used for the same purpose. Leave a book, take a book. Richard liked the idea, it smacked of an old-fashioned community spirit. The kind of thing he liked to witness from afar. But the project had got off to a rocky start in Saint-Sauver. Originally greeted with no little enthusiasm, the idea had since been sullied by person or persons unknown who had taken, presumably under the cover of darkness, to dumping decades-old pornography in there and removing some of the lighter Émile Zola novels in return. Monsieur Mabit, inevitably in charge of the project, had therefore had a lock installed on the glass cabinet and only people who were deemed trustworthy could now borrow the key. Valérie must have really worked on the petty bureaucrat to get the precious key off him then and presumably that's why Mabit was involved in the chase; he'd demanded inclusion.

Once again, Richard pulled the scarf up over his face and walked as nonchalantly as he could across the square. His phone pinged, and he didn't know whether to look at it or not. He'd never, he didn't think, seen an old *paysan* texting on a mobile phone before, and he wasn't sure if he should break character or not. But the fact that a second message arrived almost instantly meant that it was probably Valérie. The second message was the giveaway that her patience had already been tested by his tardiness in not answering the first.

Where are you? was the first message, while the second was more elaborate. *By now,* the second one began, *you will have come out of your mood. Meet me here.*

As yet, Richard had no idea where 'here' was, and it occurred to him that she was showing an awful lot of faith in his abilities and being remarkably presumptuous about his mood, even if she was spot on. He hoped he was on the right track with the *boîte à livres*. He looked around him again to make sure that no one else had, as yet, had the same epiphany. There were a few people wandering about, but none of the other players, so he casually approached the specially built, glass-covered cupboard. It was well lit and stood right outside the town hall. The key in the door was a perfect match, and he opened it with renewed confidence. The cupboard was full. There were novels galore; mainly, judging by their pastel shades, romantic ones. A few children's books, a cookery book or two and some on more local pursuits like hunting and fishing. One, a large, weighty hardback on how to hunt wild boar and another an entire book devoted to fishing knots.

'Now what?' he asked himself. He pulled out the written clue again and re-read it.

Aujourd'hui est le jour pour
vous livrer des livres.

There must be something in the clue that he'd missed, something which gave the title away. Was it a children's book? A Christmassy children's book? Was it a recipe in one of the cookery books? Surely it couldn't be the wild boar hunting? *Sanglier* meat was a local tradition on Christmas Eve, but that seemed a bit… It hit him. Christmas Eve! That's when you might deliver books. Was Eve the clue? He searched in vain for a bible, then stretched the Genesis point by looking for a book about Phil Collins. Eve? He thought next. The *Réveillon de Noël*, Christmas Eve. Or *repas*, meal, that was another word for réveillon. But there were at least half a dozen cookbooks that all looked the same, so that seemed hopeless.

He took the key out again and turned it over in his hand, searching for clues in the reflected light of the decorations. The number 24 was the obvious connection. The 24th of December, Christmas Eve. But again, nothing about the collection of books in front of him immediately suggested the number 24. There was a book on cinema, which he made a mental note to come back and borrow, and there are traditionally 24 frames per second on a standard film projection. He couldn't see Valérie setting that as a clue for some reason. Suddenly he had a brainwave! Twenty-four is the Atomic Number for... he realised he had no idea. Twenty-four carat gold? Gold, frankincense and myrrh? He was beginning to lose hope and was increasingly worried about being seen.

'Oh sod it!' he huffed, and started counting twenty-four books in from the right. Could it be the twenty-fourth book in? It seemed flimsy, but he had nothing else to go on. That turned out to be a book about fishing, which is what he felt he was now doing, albeit without success. He counted twenty-four along from the top left instead and pulled out a slim volume, *Maigret et le Marchand de Vin*. 'Maigret and the Wine Merchant' he translated automatically, then repeated it over and over again, hoping something would come to him. It didn't look like it would be the Maigret book anyway, it was in dreadful condition. The spine was falling apart, and, bizarrely, the 'i' in Maigret had been scratched out. *Why would someone do that?* he wondered. He thought about that, Maigret with no 'i'. A blind detective? That wasn't a help. No 'i' in team? He was going desperately off on a tangent, but there is an 'i' in équipe, which is French for team. *Concentrate, man.* No 'i' in Maigret. Maigret without the 'i' is Magret! Magret de Canard. She was eating Magret de Canard?

His phone beeped again. *Will you hurry up! It is very cold here.*

No. She wasn't eating duck, she was feeding them.

Chapter Six

There was a lone fisherman huddled under a large umbrella as Richard approached the bank of the River Follet. He knew immediately that it was Valérie, partly because even in the gloom, he could see that all the equipment was brand new, partly because her perfume wafted delicately in the air, which was unlike any other angler he'd ever met, partly because her outfit didn't suit the set-up and partly because Passepartout, shivering in his basket, had suddenly woken up, sensing her presence.

'Caught anything?' he asked casually as he approached.

'This really is a very dull activity, Richard. Why do people do it? Even if you catch something, you must throw it back.'

'I think people like the loneliness,' he replied. He'd been fishing once and didn't see the point either. 'That was a very clever set of clues you laid out there. Maigret with no "i". You nearly had me with that one.'

She looked up at him with a puzzled expression. 'Richard,' she said in a tone he had already learned meant that she was losing patience. 'What are you talking about?'

'The twenty-fourth book. Maigret, with the letter "i" scratched out. Magret. Canard.' He pointed at the ducks.

'The twenty-fourth book, yes. But that was a book about fishing.' She picked up a grateful Passepartout and gave him a cuddle.

He let out a deep sigh. 'Ah, well. I'm here now anyway.' He'd been very pleased with himself for working out what he thought was a devilishly clever clue, and in the end, all he'd done was count the books from the wrong end and got lucky. 'Is it dinner-time yet?' he asked, trying to change the subject.

'Not yet, there is one more round to go.' They both heard a commotion approaching along the bank, and Valérie urged Richard to swap places with her and pretend to fish. He pulled his scarf back over his face and did as he was told. The others were arriving en masse, their torch lights zipping about in front of them like a laser show; they looked like a set of pitchfork-wielding villagers hellbent on revenge for something.

'Madame,' said a red-faced duchess, 'I hope this is either the end of the game or the next clue is indoors! I am freezing.'

'We all are, Madame la Duchesse,' Comrade Rouge interrupted, showing a deference for a title that a genuine comrade wouldn't show.

'We have one more round before dinner,' Valérie said, trying to hide the fact that her own teeth were chattering. The gathered crowd grumbled in response.

Richard sat crouched under the umbrella listening to all of this; the evening gloom and, he liked to think, his disguise, meant that no one had recognised him. Either they were too obsessed with the game, or themselves, or a local *paysan* really didn't matter to them. He was thoroughly enjoying the anonymity of his presence when he felt a tugging on his fishing line. He tried to flick the rod a little, hoping that whatever was on the hook would be shaken free, but it only seemed to make the creature even more determined, flapping about on the surface somewhere in the gloom.

'Looks like you've caught something there.' Monsieur Vert stuck his head in under the umbrella and Richard mumbled an incoherent reply. 'I do miss my fishing days,' the man continued wistfully. 'There was a time when it meant the difference between eating or not. Didn't it, dear?' The dear in question, Madame la Duchesse, looked mortified by the memory and told him angrily to shut up. He looked downcast and moved in closer under Richard's umbrella. 'Cut a little slack,' he said quietly, though whether he was referring to his wife or Richard's rod technique wasn't clear.

'Madame,' Docteur Gris interrupted in his usual fashion, 'can we get on?'

'You know you're not supposed to be fishing in the dark on a river?' Monsieur Vert was happily in his own world, detached from his blousy reality. Richard again grumbled in reply. 'And I think the season legally has to finish in October.' He nudged Richard gently. 'Still, as a local, er,' he glanced at the fishing licence hanging off Richard's folding chair, 'Monsieur Battiston, you might be— Your licence is from 2015, monsieur.'

'What was that?' It was Mayor Bleu who interrupted this time. Richard had no idea if he was a real mayor or not, but he suddenly seemed very keen on the subject of localised rule-breaking.

'This fella.' Monsieur Vert stood up quickly as though disinclined to be associated with such a dastardly criminal. 'He's breaking every law in the book. The police would throw away the key!' he added, a touch dramatically.

'And there ends round one,' Valérie intervened, looking very pleased with herself.

'Very clever,' Madame Noire muttered, though she was largely ignored.

'What do you mean he's breaking every rule in the book?' The mayor wasn't letting this go.

'Well,' Monsieur Vert began, suddenly quite sheepish. 'The time of day, the time of year, the out-of-date licence. Plus he's just let that fish go.' Richard felt his line go slack.

Docteur Gris pushed back the umbrella revealing Richard and his inadequate disguise. 'You!' Gris shouted. 'I knew it! So who are you then?' He rounded on poor Monsieur Mabit, who despite hiding behind his 'elves' fell backwards in terror.

'That is quite enough!' It was Madame Noire who stood between her partner and the prostrate Papa Noël. She shone a torch at Valérie and said, with an air of fatigue, 'Shall we get on, madame? Now that round one is complete.'

Some twenty minutes later, the group had reconvened in the town centre. Tempers had calmed a little, but there was a general air of suspicion especially, Richard felt, towards him and his dubious appearance as a renegade fisherman. Poor Monsieur Mabit had had enough too and had gone home, after asking Valérie's permission, which was granted on the understanding that she didn't like to have odd numbers at a dinner table. He'd obsequiously thanked her anyway for 'allowing him to take part' and shot Richard a look that was angry, defeated and 'you're welcome to her mate' all in one go. Martin and Gennie for their part looked permanently distracted as though they had other plans, and all the invited couples appeared to have come together as one team, which was apparently against the rules, and were directing their increasing air of revolution at both Valérie and Richard. And while Richard was happy to be associated with Valérie in almost any way, if pressed he'd have admitted that he hadn't a clue what was going on. So, he'd been caught fishing without a licence; how did Madame Noire conclude that was round one over and done with?

'Help yourself to a glass of *vin chaud*,' Valérie said helpfully as the teams stamped their feet and huddled for warmth. A small table had been set up at the end of the rue des Soeurs, and, along with *vin chaud*, there was a selection of other drinks and snacks. Madame Noire already had a glass in hand, and Monsieur Vert, while still eyeing Richard as a diabolical reprobate, was helping to serve. 'Now,' Valérie's voice rose against the hubbub and the background noise of the town. 'Papa Noël has gone home to prepare for a busy night,' she said with an awkward, unpractised, levity.

'Why did you switch Papa Noël?' It was the duchess who asked, though Richard had some sympathy for the question.

'I ordered the wrong sized costume,' Valérie's reply had the cold monotone of a self-service supermarket check-out. 'It did not fit Richard, so the other gentlemen agreed to step in.'

This half explanation left Richard with the uncomfortable realisation that he was now the only one not anonymous.

'Can I go home too?' he whimpered.

'No Richard, you are to read out the next set of clues.' She gave him a pleading look that was a damned sight more practised than her levity, and devastatingly effective.

'And then we eat?' Docteur Gris had softened a little since Madame Noire had faced him down on the riverbank, but he still had a need to be heard.

'Then we eat,' Valérie replied.

'Indoors?' Madame la Duchesse asked.

'Then we eat, indoors.' Richard could see that Valérie's patience was wearing thin. She handed Richard an envelope, and he started to read out the instructions.

'This is the picture round,' he said, raising his voice. He cleared his throat and continued:

If you stand, with drink in hand
and look towards the light.
There are six clues
Of differing hues,
that show the power and the might.

He read it aloud again, more slowly. Then read it to
himself, more quickly. Docteur Gris insisted that he
read it for himself, and the duchess asked Monsieur
Vert to work it out for them. Comrade Rouge did as
she was instructed by the poem, Mayor Bleu the same
and Madame Noire helped herself to another glass.
Martin and Gennie huddled in a doorway like two
teenagers about to grope each other in a bus shelter.

'If you look towards the light,' Comrade Rouge said,
thinking aloud, 'presumably that means the church.
God is the light.'

They all turned to look at the brightly lit church.
There was the gentle sound of a choir coming from
within. Richard was not a religious man himself and
he couldn't have vouched for any of the odd collective
around him, but the image and the music moved him
nevertheless. It was true also that from the corner of
the rue des Soeurs, you could see much of the town.
All the shops, to the left and to the right, were lit up
and decorated, their warmth lighting up the evening
sky, trying to entice some last-minute purchases before closing finally for Christmas. Among the shops
were the *presse*, with its Christmas magazines, books,
DVDs and the latest newspaper headlines; the chemist

with tinsel wrapped around its window display of zimmer frames and orthopaedic socks. The inevitable optician, of which every small French town had at least three, the hairdresser, the café-bar, the new 'sell your unwanted gold shop', called *Achat d'Or*. Run by the same man, it had recently replaced the short-lived vape shop, though Richard didn't fancy the chances of the new venture either. *This is Saint-Sauver,* he could have told him. *There aren't many inhabitants with unwanted gold.* On the corner and long-since closed for the day was Grossard et Fils, the furniture-maker, who specialised in overpriced wooden floors and kitchen units and whose own building was being renovated, so with the iron scaffolding it looked like a scaled-down Pompidou Centre.

'I have to say,' it was the duchess who broke the silence, 'that church is beautiful.' She seemed a little cowed by it. 'Those stained-glass windows, especially. Who is the saint in the windows, madame?'

The question was directed at Valérie, but it was a slurring Madame Noire who answered. 'That is King Solomon,' she said, before adding, 'dispensing judgement.' The way she said it had an effect on the group. That it must be one of the clues seemed to be the general consensus, and they turned to Valérie for her own judgement.

'Five to go,' she said flatly.

Everybody started to look in different directions now; the air of competition had returned and even Martin and Gennie were back in the spirit.

'There's a lot going on in the newsagent's window,' Martin offered. 'Something in a headline, maybe?' A train strike was planned for the new year, which seemed neither helpful nor, this being France, news.

'*L'Achat d'Or*?' Monsieur Vert avoided the duchess's withering glance as he nervously said the words.

'What are you talking about?' she said anyway, and, despite him revealing Richard's disguise at the riverbank, he felt sorry for the man.

'Well…' Monsieur Vert gulped and decided to carry on, 'You have Solomon, Solomon the wise, dispenser of justice and—'

'And what?'

'And the shop has a picture of scales in the window, for weighing gold.'

'The scales of justice,' Richard finished the sentence before the man broke down completely.

'Pah!' The duchess snorted.

'Four to go!' Valérie shouted. 'Well done, Monsieur Vert.'

Richard thought that might cheer the man up, but instead he had a look of fear on his face that suggested there'd be retribution for his impertinence.

'I have a feeling about the optician's…' Docteur Gris didn't like being left out of anything and was clearly doing a bit of fishing of his own.

'The All-Seeing Eye, you mean?' It was Martin who volunteered this information and surprised everyone by doing so. 'It's a Masonic symbol, I think. God sees everything, that sort of thing. So it's a justice thing as well.'

'Well done, Martin!' Gennie cried, and kissed him on the cheek.

Everyone waited for Valérie to declare that as number three, but, much to Martin's disappointment, she stayed silent.

'No dice, old girl?' Martin asked, hoping to change her mind. 'Shame that.'

'It is not the eye,' le Maire Bleu's voice was quiet and steady, working things out as he went along. 'It's the *lunettes.*'

'Glasses?' Gennie was out to defend her man.

'No, madame, a different kind of *lunette* and a different kind of justice. The guillotine.' He rolled his tongue around the last word to give it an extra, chilling effect.

'That's correct!' Comrade Rouge was trying to steal her partner's thunder. 'The *lunette* on a guillotine was the stock where the…'

'…where the condemned put their head for the last time,' Bleu finished quickly and shot a false smile at Comrade Rouge, who pretended not to see it.

'Three left!' said Valérie.

'Look, can we hurry up, please?' Madame la Duchesse was out of her depth and not remotely interested any more. 'Or I might be the victim you are searching for; death from hypothermia.'

'Three left,' Valérie repeated, ignoring the woman.

'I still think there's got to be something in the newsagent's window.' It was Martin, inevitably, who broke the silence. 'There's a few magazines in there that deal with punishment!' He winked at Gennie, who giggled. In an effort to offer a palette cleanser to that image, Richard spoke up.

'Is that *The Aristocats* DVD in the window? Late period, classic Disney, but always worth a look. Maurice Chevalier was in it,' he added, trying to impress the French contingent.

'Oh, I love that film!' Gennie said.

Madame Noire was having none of this distraction. 'I see the point of *lunette*, madame,' she addressed Valérie directly. 'But that is not justice, that is execution.'

Valérie smiled back, acknowledging the point. 'You are correct, madame. The six clues are divided into two groups of three.'

This caused some murmuring and disquiet in the group, who clearly felt it was a bit late to be informed of this. Madame Noire nodded silently, or she really had overdone it on the drink, but her voice actually seemed to be getting clearer with each glass she put away. 'Then I would say the furniture-maker is the obvious next choice.'

Valérie smiled, 'That, as madame has cleverly surmised, leaves two.'

This time the following silence was a stunned one. 'How?' Docteur Gris was not only unconvinced by the connection, but also obviously didn't like Madame Noire constantly getting the better of everyone.

'Does he build guillotines?' Martin asked. 'A specialist who builds to instructions?' Richard couldn't even begin to think what the degenerate had in mind now.

'I've got it!' Comrade Rouge briefly let her coolness drop. 'The scaffolding. It represents the scaffold. The executioner's scaffold.'

'Bravo, madame.' Valérie looked keenly at the group. 'Like I say, that leaves two.'

'Is *The Aristocats* on this Christmas, Richard?' Gennie seemed keen to move away from the topic of death. 'I love that song "Everybody Wants to Be a Cat". I've got a cat—' Martin made as if to say something, but she cut him short. 'Not now, dear,' she said.

Richard was happy for the distraction too, mainly because the one clue he had worked out in the whole game so far he had entirely misinterpreted and had got absolutely nowhere near any of the others. 'Interesting thing about that film,' he said, not really bothered if anyone was listening or not. 'It was the last thing Chevalier ever did.'

Only Valérie paid this comment any real attention. 'That leaves one!' she said to the astonishment of the group. 'Well done, Richard!'

Again, it was a sort of vexed chattering that greeted Valérie's outburst. 'What are you talking about now?' Docteur Gris, it was now clear to everyone, had serious anger management issues.

The solution came from a surprising source. 'Chevalier,' Madame la Duchesse said, affecting her poshest accent, 'Marcel Chevalier was the last executioner in France.' She looked around triumphantly. 'I read it in a magazine.'

'Correct, madame. That still leaves one more.'

Everybody looked around, a sense of fierce rivalry hanging in the air, not so much between the teams but more within them.

'I can't see anything,' Monsieur Vert said desperately, and his wife tutted at him.

'Well, while we wait for inspiration,' Madame Noire was at her most serious, 'can I inform you that we have run out of wine.'

Honestly, the woman was a solid gold lush, thought Richard and offered to pour her something else. 'Hang on.' He turned to Valérie, a bottle of yellow liquid in his hand. 'This is my nan's bottle of Advocaat? Did you take my nan's bottle of Advocaat out of my drinks cabinet? That's been in the family for nearly forty years!' Everybody looked at him as though the cold might have got to his brain. 'It's a British tradition,' he added defensively. 'Every family in Britain has a bottle of something nasty that emerges at Christmas and remains undrunk.' It didn't help. 'It's usually Advocaat.'

'And that is number six. Brilliant, Richard!'

'What?' Docteur Gris was practically foaming at the mouth. 'What has a vile Dutch liqueur got to do with it?'

'Say it quickly,' Valérie ordered.

'Ah, Advocaat for *avocat*,' le Maire Bleu couldn't help smiling. 'Advocaat, *avocat*. A lawyer, you mean?'

'That's a bit obtuse, isn't it?' Comrade Rouge seemed put out.

'Nevertheless, it fits. *Avocat*, lawyer. Justice.' Madame Noire, as usual, seemed one step ahead of everyone else.

61

The large wooden door behind the drinks table suddenly opened with a sinister creak, startling the duchess especially. Even more so when a nun, not much shy of six feet, emerged, her pure white habit and wimple almost ghostly in the frosty night air. '*À table*,' the nun said gracefully, 'dinner is served.'

Chapter Seven

Richard couldn't help looking at Valérie questioningly. He had no idea if he'd been brilliant by accident, brilliant by design or if the infernal woman had just spotted a quick way to end the game because it was getting chilly. He also couldn't help but notice that the volatile Docteur Gris was giving him the skunk eye again as if Richard had known the answers all along and had just been toying with them. What's more, and he couldn't help this either, the convent made him feel uneasy. It was all getting a bit spooky, all a bit *Da Vinci Code* for his tastes, plus he hadn't even known that the place existed.

The interior of the 'restaurant', if that's what it was, was all low-ceiling cloisters and stone pillars with what looked like thousands of candles acting as the only light. The shadows of the group as they filed in looked enormous and menacing on the curved walls climbing, Nosferatu-like, into grotesque silhouettes. Everybody became quiet as soon as they realised that their voices were amplified and echoed around the stone chambers, their chatter dying down so that the only noise was the quiet music coming from speakers dotted about. Richard had no objection to Gregorian Christmas chants; under normal circumstances and given a choice of Christmas music, he would certainly have taken them over Slade and Cliff Richard, but in this environment they sounded baleful, threatening almost, and he wondered if Valérie had confused Christmas with Halloween.

They made their way nervously to a slightly bigger central chamber in which a large, circular dining table dressed for the ten guests was sat in the middle, with even more candles adorning the simple holly centrepiece. At each place there were name cards showing where people should sit, and it was noticeable that, apart from Richard and Valérie, all the couples had been deliberately split up. Richard sat down first, still in a daze and still trying to figure things out. He looked around at the characters in the room. This was like one of those big production Agatha Christie films; everyone had a secret and a motive. Though, as yet, he couldn't see a crime or a victim, just a group of fairly unpleasant people tempted out on Christmas Eve purely by greed.

While everybody took their place, the shadows still bouncing menacingly in the candlelight, Madame Noire remained standing, just.

'I have something to say,' she said, a stoic defiance in her voice. 'The first part of this so-called game, I take it, is over.' She looked directly at Valérie, who nodded in response. 'Government,' Madame Noire said simply.

'What do you mean, "government"?' The duchess was already tucking her napkin into her pearls.

'I mean, Madame la Duchesse,' the address wasn't delivered kindly, 'that government is the key. Our task was to identify a victim, and a motive. And eventually, I believe, a murderer also.'

'And you believe that government, the state, is the murderer, madame?' Monsieur le Bleu seemed energised by the thought.

Madame Noire leaned her tired head to one side. 'Solomon, scales, *avocat*. The judicial arm of government.'

'Chevalier, *lunette* and scaffolding is the executive!' Docteur Gris had a look of such triumph on his thin face you'd have thought he'd discovered the secret of alchemy.

'So,' said Monsieur Vert, who obviously felt emboldened by not sitting next to his wife, though he carefully avoided her eye nonetheless, 'all the broken fishing rules, that's the legislative?'

'Precisely, monsieur. Legislative, Judicial and Executive. Government.'

'All that charade of keys, books and fishing, just to show the legislative arm of government?' Docteur Gris snorted. 'That's even more dubious than Advocaat/ *avocat*!'

'Well, I still don't get it,' the duchess barked, looking around for service.

Madame Noire sat down slowly. 'I am tired,' she said quietly, 'so I will begin the next round, if madame will permit me?' She looked at Valérie, who nodded her consent. 'You will not be surprised to learn that I am not an undertaker; I am a judge on the Court of Cassation.'

'The highest court in France,' Docteur Gris added as if the power would rub off on him.

'We are supposed to maintain our anonymity!' The duchess looked horrified that she might lose her claim on the legacy.

'I no longer care for that.' Madame Noire shrugged her off. 'You may do what you like.' She leaned forward, putting a shaky elbow on the table. 'If you don't though, you might not get the prize!' She laughed, looking with confrontation around the table, to see if anyone else dared the same.

'But what do you mean, madame, the government?' It was le Maire Bleu who asked the question after a pause; no doubt talk of the legislature involved him too in some way, Richard thought, as a mayor, if he was a mayor.

'I do not know yet, Monsieur le Maire, I am thinking aloud, that is all. But if the victim or motive are the three sovereign arms of government Legislative, Executive…'

'Judicial!' shrieked the duchess like it was a pub quiz.

'…then I declare my interest now.' Madame Noire ignored her. 'I doubt I am alone.'

'I, too, will declare an interest.' Comrade Rouge ran a finger around the rim of her glass and, Richard noticed, looked fleetingly at Valérie. 'I am not a Communist agitator, nor am I a union representative; I work in the

Ministry of the Interior.' Her eyes suddenly looked very sad. 'I used my position to threaten my ex-husband. I used government, if that is the word we are using, rather than position or power, and promised to make his life a bureaucratic hell if he refused to divorce me. He is a brutish man, violent, and I used the only weapon I had. I could have changed his identity, added points to his driving licence, removed his licence, changed his address or given him a criminal record. I could even have declared him dead. I am not ashamed of what I did, but I know it was wrong.'

'It's not possible to just declare someone's dead!' The red-faced duchess may have been out of her depth, but Richard sympathised with her point.

'That's right,' he added. 'Surely you need a death certificate at least?' He didn't ask this with total confidence, knowing his own run-ins with the dreaded French state.

'Not always.' Docteur Gris had a nasty look on his face. 'Sometimes, all you need is the right *avocat.*' He sounded like he was touting for business. 'But don't look at me,' he added, 'I was thrown out of law school!'

A silence fell on the table which was broken suddenly by the tall nun who had let them in, and who was evidently the Mother Superior. *'Mesdames et messieurs,'* she said loudly, *'les entrées.'* Two other nuns followed her in, wheeling a trolley containing a large soup terrine, and Richard took the opportunity to whisper in Valérie's ear.

'Valérie?'

'Yes?' She smiled without looking at him.

'What the bloody hell is going on?'

'I was going to ask that.' Martin looked around from the other side of Valérie. 'Buggered if I know!' he added.

'Has it finished yet?' Gennie asked from the other side of Richard.

'Oh! Look what you've done!' the duchess shrieked from across the table. 'How am I supposed to get pumpkin soup out of jacquard silk?'

There followed an awkward pause as everyone reflected on whether they had ever seen a nun shouted at before. The poor woman, much stouter than her Mother Superior, kept her head down and mumbled softly, 'I'll pray for you, madame,' before scuttling off.

'I'm a duchess, not a madame!' the duchess shouted after her before turning back to the table where everyone else seemed to have a spoon halfway between their bowls and their mouths. 'What?' the duchess asked, the picture of innocence.

Monsieur Vert, from the relative safety of having Comrade Rouge and Docteur Gris between himself and his wife, was now attacking the wine with gusto and beginning to feel emboldened. 'You never did like sisters, did you, dear?' he said, the look on his face suggesting he was genuinely trying to lighten the atmosphere.

'Shut up!' was his wife's reply, and the man's head sunk into his neck like a startled tortoise.

'If she's a duchess,' Martin leaned around Valérie again, 'then I'm Diana Ross.'

'I must remind you,' Valérie spoke with authority, 'it is against the rules to reveal our true identities.' There was a quiet murmur. 'However, I am the arbiter of such things, and I don't think that now it is much of a problem.'

The nuns reappeared with their serving trollies while the Mother Superior refilled the wine glasses. Monsieur Vert picked up his glass and stared into it mournfully. 'My identity doesn't really matter,' he said dolefully. 'I'm retired, so chauffeur, isn't far off the mark. It's about all I do anyway.'

'It's about all you ever did,' the duchess said, though her heart wasn't in the venom of her comment. 'We, or should I say I, ran a successful family cleaning business.' She looked defiantly around the room. 'But it folded.'

'I am not a mayor,' Monsieur Bleu said, happy, it seemed, to lose the weight of office. 'I am a *Sécretaire National* for the CGT union. Specifically, I head the department for *fonctionnaires*, civil servants.'

'Then I'm surprised you made it this far without going on strike!' Docteur Gris joked.

'And what is it that you do that is so worthy, monsieur?' was the immediate response.

'Worthy?' The younger man smiled. 'I do nothing. Worthy or otherwise. I am a kept man, aren't I, my dear?' He directed a thin smile at Madame Noire, who didn't look overjoyed to be reminded of the situation.

'Yes,' she said simply. 'Though not for much longer.' If this was news to Docteur Gris, he didn't show it.

'I swear I cannot keep up with all this,' Gennie said, shaking her head, and Richard had some sympathy with her, but that wasn't going to stop Martin from getting involved.

'I run a correctional institution with my wife!' he said, very pleased with himself.

Full plates were placed in front of each person, and the delicious smell interrupted the flow of the conversation.

'*Filet mignon de porc en croûte farci au pain d'épices et morilles*,' the Mother Superior intoned, as if it were an act of God in itself. 'The sisters will serve a jus of parmesan and mustard. *Bon appétit!*'

Valérie stood up, tapping her glass to get everyone's attention. 'Before we begin,' she said, 'I want to thank everyone for taking part. I think we are nearer the solution to this puzzle, but,' she bent down and picked up a cardboard box, 'we still have a few points to address.' She opened the box and produced a Christmas cracker.

'Oh,' Gennie exclaimed, 'how delightful!'

'What is it?' Docteur Gris asked suspiciously.

'It's a Christmas cracker,' Richard said, finally having had enough of the man's attitude. 'It's a British Christmas tradition, and it's fun, so there's two reasons why you'd hate it!'

'That's a given,' the younger man was not in the least put off, 'but *what* is it?'

'It's a cracker!' Martin beamed. 'You pull it! It makes a sound like a, like a *pétard*, those things that everyone throws around on Bastille Day, and then there's a toy, a paper hat and a joke inside!' He said all of this with the confidence of a man who knew that the explanation just could not fail to impress and that the docteur would love every second of it. 'Look, I'll show you.' He took a cracker out of the box and pointed it at Gennie. 'I'll hold my end, dear, give it a good pull, will you?' Richard groaned audibly.

The report of the cracker startled a few at the table, but the docteur remained unimpressed.

'Look,' Gennie said, 'I've won some nail clippers.' She put her paper crown on her head and unfurled the small paper with the joke on it. 'Which sea do zombies swim in?' she asked the unimpressed room. Nobody proffered an answer. 'The Dead Sea!' she cried, then her face fell. 'Well, it's also a sort of tradition that the jokes aren't very good,' she explained apologetically.

'You see?' Martin asked the docteur, who remained impassive.

'Can we eat now?' he asked as a nun ladled some jus onto his plate.

'I'll pull one with you,' Monsieur Vert said, addressing the former Comrade Rouge. The woman, who had remained relatively frosty throughout the day, seemed more relaxed since her admission of attempted bureaucratic assassination and eagerly accepted. They pulled the cracker, giggling as they did so, and it was Monsieur Vert who won. Graciously he gave away the prize of a tailor's measuring tape, but kept the paper hat which he wore at a rakish angle.

'And the joke?' Gennie asked, hoping it was better than her effort.

Comrade Rouge picked it up. 'What would you call an undead cheese?' she asked, a look of confusion on her face.

'Zom-Brie,' Madame Noire said with a wan smile. 'I think I am beginning to see a pattern here. Bravo, madame.' She raised a glass towards Valérie.

'What do you mean, a pattern?' asked the duchess impatiently.

'The undead, Madame la Duchesse.'

'Is somebody not dead, you mean? Does that mean we don't inherit anything?'

The nun beside her poured the jus onto the duchess's plate and then very slowly and very deliberately continued pouring into the woman's lap.

'What on earth are you doing now, you stupid woman?' The duchess rose to her feet, holding the pose of a prize-fighter. 'You did that on purpose! Get me a cloth immediately!' The nun's face was in the shadow of her wimple, which she now removed and handed as a cloth to the startled woman.

'You?' The duchess collapsed back into her chair, her face a picture of shock.

Monsieur Vert intervened. 'But you're dead!' he cried, before noticing that the nun was pointing a small pistol at his wife.

Chapter Eight

'Blanche,' Valérie said calmly and deliberately. 'This is not the way to do this.'

Nobody looked to Valérie for an explanation as they were all concentrating on the small gun in the shaky hand of the now wimple-less nun. Those that had stood up in shock now slowly sat down again, careful not to make any sudden movements. It took a moment for Richard to make the connection too; Blanche, the tramp at the charity clothing box and who he'd left drunkenly asleep on his cinema room floor. He hadn't recognised her at first, but it was fair to say she scrubbed up pretty well for a down and out, certainly an inebriated one, and even more certainly a dead one. So she was the killer Valérie was hunting? Well, he might have been informed, he thought, not a little put out at having been left alone in a confined space with the rum-soaked, gun-toting menace.

'This isn't the way to do this, is it not?' the old woman sneered. 'Why not? I'm dead, remember? How are they going to arrest me, a dead woman? They would have to give me my life back to do that, and that would be worth it alone.'

'But we've got your ashes on our mantelpiece!' Monsieur Vert wasn't the only one struggling with the mechanics of the situation.

'Of course, she's not Blanche,' the shaken duchess said without conviction. 'It's just an actress. Blanche is dead.'

'Yes,' Blanche said sadly. 'Blanche is dead. Because you had me killed.'

'Can someone please explain what is going on?' The former Mayor Bleu, actually a high-up union rep and therefore someone who should have had a better grasp of Byzantine entanglements, shook his head in confusion.

'I think we should possibly remove the gun first,' Madame Noire said, without taking her eyes off the alive dead woman.

'And you?' Blanche started waving the gun in the direction of the colourless and obviously scared Docteur Gris. 'You normally have plenty to say, lost your tongue?'

Again, without taking his eyes from the woman, he said, with a panicky edge to his voice, 'I've never seen this woman before, I swear it!'

Nobody had noticed Valérie move stealthily around the table, but she now appeared at the old woman's side. She put one arm tenderly around Blanche's shoulder, hugging the woman into her and with her right hand held the old lady's wrist, almost caressing it until it went limp and the gun fell gently into Valérie's palm.

She put the gun in her own pocket, led Blanche to the other side of the table and put her gently into her chair, next to Richard.

Docteur Gris stood up immediately. 'Right, I'm calling the police. I want this lunatic arrested immediately.'

'I agree!' The duchess had her confidence back also. 'Making false accusations like that. She's probably drunk, they usually are.'

'Who are, nuns?' Richard couldn't help himself.

'No, vagrants!' The duchess was full of spite now.

'How did you know she was a vagrant?' Valérie posed the question quietly, but also like wielding a sharp knife.

'Be quiet, please, just be quiet.' It was Madame Noire who intervened and addressed both the duchess and Docteur Gris, 'Or I swear I'll use that gun myself.' The docteur sat back down again, a look of shock on his face.

'Madame.' Valérie filled Blanche's glass with water. 'Please tell us your story.'

'It'll be a pack of lies, whatever it is!' The duchess hitched up her bosom in annoyance.

'Shut up!' It was Monsieur Vert who had finally turned the tables. 'I want to hear this.'

'Well!' The duchess looked around for sympathy and support, but again she found none.

Blanche Noel took a large gulp of water and smoothed out her habit. 'I don't know where to start,' she began quietly. 'I don't even know how it started, all I know is how it ended. It ended in my death.'

'Oh, this is ridiculous!' Docteur Gris exclaimed. 'The woman's mad!'

'No,' Valérie said firmly, 'she is not mad. Driven to the brink of insanity possibly, but not mad, no.' Valérie had a way of putting a slight tone in her voice that not only stopped aggressive males in their tracks, but which would probably halt a wildebeest migration. 'Remember madame here,' she acknowledged the former Comrade Rouge, 'she told us that she had threatened her ex-husband. That with access to personal files in the Ministry of the Interior, she could ruin someone's life?'

'So she's the guilty one then!' the duchess wailed.

'No.' Again Valérie was calm. 'Madame Rouge is here at my invitation, as a witness. As is monsieur.' She nodded towards Monsieur Bleu, the union man. 'Please go on, Blanche.'

With obvious pain and difficulty, Blanche Noel began her story. 'It began at the doctor's,' she said. 'I used to go regularly for my arthritis, and to have my prescription renewed. But the docteur said that my Carte Vitale, you know my health card, she said it wasn't working. I thought nothing of it at first, even though I had to pay for my medicines at the chemist because of the same problem. Just some technical thing, I thought, I'll get the money back. Then I tried to renew my passport, but that was refused as well. Then I noticed that my bank account was emptying, even though I was paying in cheques. The bank manager, who I've known for years, said that my account no longer existed, that I no longer existed. But I'm here, I told him. I know, he said. But the computer says that you aren't.' She looked around the table. 'Someone had declared me dead. My driving licence, my *carte d'identité*, my home, all of it was taken away. I am alive, you can see that?' It was almost a plea for confirmation. 'But officially, I am dead.'

Madame Rouge shook her head. 'It is possible,' she said, 'remember, I thought of doing that to my ex.'

The effect on the table was marked. The duchess was trying to keep up appearances until the end, defiantly staring back. Docteur Gris was nervously toying with his cutlery, and Madame Noire looked downcast. 'Sometimes,' Valérie said quietly, 'all you need is the right *avocat*. That's what you told us, Docteur Gris.'

'But I am not an *avocat*, I really was thrown out of law school.' He said this with a sly look on his face, as if his failure made him untouchable.

'Sometimes, madame, all you need is the right judge.' Madame Noire sighed heavily and shifted in her seat. She turned to her younger partner. The colour had now completely drained from the face of Docteur Gris. 'I was besotted by you,' she said with a cracked voice. 'Him,' she added more sternly addressing the rest of the group. 'No debt was too great that I wouldn't pay it off for him. Then he came up with a scheme to make money, which we both needed. He would involve some former law school friends, ones that could be bought, and have them take on litigation cases or employment tribunals.' Docteur Gris stood quickly but the Mother Superior, now showing a surprising number of angry tattoos on her forearms, pushed him back down again.

Madame Noire continued, 'Sometimes cases drag on for years, but if you declare the plaintiff dead, you can, under some circumstances, take their assets. Like I say,' she went on very quietly, 'all you really need is a compliant judge to agree to a declaration of death, that's it, no proof even. And the wheels of the state, legislative, judicial and executive, do the rest. I am so sorry, madame. I killed you.' A tear fell on Blanche's cheek, but she said nothing. 'I don't have long left,' Madame Noire was now almost pleading. 'But whatever I can do to turn this around, I will.'

'I didn't think it would actually happen!' the duchess wailed and looked around again for support. 'I thought it would just be a joke! Tell them!' She looked at her husband, begging him for help, but Monsieur Vert wasn't looking at her.

'My dear sister-in-law, Blanche, I thought you were dead,' he said, with genuine sorrow. 'She told me you were dead and that you'd been cremated.'

'You know adultery is a sin!' The Duchess was wild with anger and lost power.

'But we weren't adulterous!' Monsieur Vert had tears in his eyes. 'We just had a common enemy.'

'She ruined our business, my business!' The duchess was now fiercely angry, pointing at Blanche. 'I couldn't sack her, she was part owner, but her carelessness cost me my position. I had so many tribunals to deal with because she screwed up contracts, employees who took *me* to court for her mistakes. She deserved it, I'm telling you. What about me?'

'How?' Richard couldn't help himself. He'd be the first one to admit that if any country could commit murder via clerical error it was France, but why and bloody how?

'How what?' the duchess replied petulantly. 'How did she destroy our, *my*, company. She employed vagrants, monsieur, unlicensed immigrants. She signed contracts on their behalf, set up false bank accounts, paid them cash and paid their *unpaid* taxes into charities.' The table took this in silently. 'I mean that's wrong isn't it?' There was no reply. 'Wrong.'

'How did you take your revenge, madame?' Valérie asked quietly.

'Les Dames Qui Fait,' she said, momentarily wistful.

Richard perked up at this and whispered in Valérie's ear, 'Ladies Who Do,' he said. She gave him a look that quite reasonably questioned why he was translating the French for her. '*Ladies Who Do*,' he repeated. '1963. Robert Morley, Peggy Mount...' Her look became more withering. 'Harry H. Corbett...' He tailed off.

'I put our business solely in her name.' The duchess had regained her ire. 'It was easy to forge her signature for business contracts and even pretend to be her if necessary.' She pointed at her sister. 'I thought I'd see how she liked the responsibility and the cost and especially the debts. I even set something else up without her, became a competitor. Then I heard about this scheme. A lawyer approached me; one of *his* lot, no doubt.' She pointed at Gris. 'I could pay them to recover the debts they said, by declaring her dead. They had a friendly judge.' She shrugged, as if it was nothing to do with her. 'For a fee obviously. And I thought, why not? I've lost everything, anyway, let her have the same fate.' A vicious smile broke out across her face. 'Anyway, you can't arrest me, she's dead. How does she press any charges?'

Docteur Gris looked up. 'That's right, isn't it, mad-ame?' He looked around the table. 'This is all very interesting, good Christmas fun and games, but the woman is dead. She can't call the police; she has no ID to make any accusation against us. And if she says that we murdered her, as she's claiming, they'll say that she's obviously alive!'

Richard looked at Valérie pleadingly, wondering if this was true, if these vile people really were going to get away with murder, even if it wasn't murder, more a murderless murder, the victim still being alive and all.

'Alas,' Valérie said quietly and moved back around the table to stand behind Blanche. 'You are correct. As things stand, Blanche is still dead.' She looked almost defeated.

'Fill my glass, will you?' Docteur Gris demanded of the Mother Superior.

'And mine.' The duchess had restored her poshest accent. The two of them clinked glasses from across the table.

'Is this really it?' Richard asked Valérie. 'Is there nothing we can do?'

'It seems not.'

'Bugger.'

'Richard, just lean into that box, will you? It is Christmas, Blanche deserves something at least.'

A confused Richard rummaged in the box and picked up a small, beautifully wrapped gift. On it were ribbons and bows and snowmen and a smiling Papa Noël himself. He gave the present to Valérie.

'Merry Christmas, Blanche,' she said, passing the gift across to the old woman. 'I hope this helps in some way.'

Blanche nervously took the package, a look of bewilderment and resignation on her face. Slowly she undid the ribbons and, careful not to tear the paper, unwrapped the present. Inside was a brown A5 envelope. Again, she looked at Valérie before opening the flap. She poured the contents onto the table in front of her. There was a driving licence, a *Carte Vitale*, a passport, even a library card. Tears rolled down her face as she picked up the driving licence and touched first the miniature photo of herself and then guided her finger gently across her name, Blanche Noel. She clutched the licence to her bosom. 'I'm alive,' she said softly as a tear rolled down her cheek.

'Thank you for your help, madame.' Valérie nodded to the elegant former Comrade Rouge. 'Now, could you call the police?'

Richard and Valérie walked across the market square later that evening. Arrests had been made; even though Docteur Gris had insisted that Blanche's documents must be fake, the woman from the Ministry of the Interior was on hand to authenticate their validity, so Blanche was most definitely alive. Madame Noire was arrested too and immediately confirmed that she would tell everything she knew about Docteur Gris and his 'organisation'. Even the duchess was arrested, though admittedly on shakier legal ground, as she was accused of killing someone who was most definitely alive.

'I'm still not sure I understand all of this,' Richard confessed as they walked in the chilly moonlight. 'Will any of those people actually be found guilty of anything?'

Valérie thought about this for a second. 'I think so, yes. Fraud, conspiracy…'

'But not murder?'

'No,' she said flatly. 'Not of murder.'

'Well that feels wholly unsatisfying.' Richard stiffened his shoulders and clenched his jaw. 'It doesn't feel right at all. They murdered Blanche.' He furrowed his brow. 'Sort of.'

'I agree Richard, but Blanche will not be the only victim. There will be others I fear, more walking dead, their lives destroyed by petty rivalry and a legal loophole.'

'So there'll be more arrests then?' Richard needed some kind of closure and also comfort.

'Twenty-two arrests were made this afternoon Richard. A criminal network broken, their lives will be ruined and other people's lives will be restored, if they can be found.'

Richard sighed in admiration and shook his head. 'Well that is good news. I hope they're found guilty of whatever it is they've done!' he said with typical understatement.

Not for the first time Valérie giggled at his Englishness. 'They will be. Sometimes, Richard, all you need is the right judge…' she added enigmatically.

They walked on in silence for a minute or two. 'So, you arranged all of that? Right down to the clues and so on.' Richard was still in a bit of a whirl about the whole thing.

'I had help with the clues,' Valérie admitted. 'An old friend does that kind of thing for a living.'

'And Blanche?'

'I met her in Paris. She was asleep in my doorway, and I brought her in. She told me her story, so I did some digging.'

'That's quite a Christmas present, you know. To give someone their life back, I mean.' They walked on.

'So, who is, was, this Sacha Bevellini?'

'I made them up.'

'But the duchess said she had done the online research, that this thing was an annual event.'

'Richard, as you can make a life disappear, it is just as easy to create a new one. Madame Noire saw through it, I think, but she was happy, finally, to have it resolved.'

'Saw through what, Sacha Bevellini?'

Valérie chuckled. 'Do you like anagrams, Richard?'

He groaned, 'No. Not really. And I certainly couldn't work it out without a pen and paper.' They walked on in silence as Richard tried to work it out in his head anyway. Eventually, he gave up, making a mental note to return to it later.

He shook his head. 'And the nuns?'

'Hired guns, I think you'd call them. Oh, Richard!' she said, stopping suddenly and looking to the heavens.

Her sudden change of mood unnerved him and he looked about nervously for more hired guns. 'What?' he asked in a small panic.

'It is beginning to snow, look!' Small flakes were falling onto the ground, with a bigger flurry soon following. 'I love Christmas!' Valérie said, opening her arms wide to catch the snow.

'Well, we'd better get on and enjoy it then, you only have one day of it in this country!'

'But, Richard,' she replied enigmatically. 'Christmas isn't just a day, it's a frame of mind.'

'What?' He couldn't believe what he had just heard. 'You're quoting *Miracle on 34th Street* at me? You know that film?'

'Honestly, no.' She put her arm through his. 'But if I am to come here more often, I thought I'd do some film research.'

He was at a complete loss for words.

'Now, Richard,' she added seriously, putting Passepartout in his arms. 'If we hurry, it is on BBC2 at 11.30 tonight. I take it you have the DVD ready?'

Preview

Death at the Chateau

(A Follet Valley Mystery 3)

Chapter One

The sun was a quarter way over the horizon, its weak, early morning beams just beginning to flood the distant Follet Valley like a transfusion of blood, giving the place life. It was mid-September and for Richard Ainsworth, the best time of the year for this usually quiet corner of the wider Loire Valley. The mist that clung like cobwebs to the trees and the fattening vines would be burnt off by late morning, and the day would be as warm and languorous as at the height of summer, only without the tourist crowds – allowing the locals to reclaim their quiet land.

But that would be late morning, still half the day away. Richard had no trouble with early mornings: as the owner of a high-end *chambre d'hôte*, or 'posh B&B' as one of his recent guests had called it, causing a small part of him to die inside, an ability to get up early was the most basic of qualifications. What was unusual about today though was the enthusiasm with which he had bounced out of bed, almost causing himself to rick his neck in the process. Today was the first day on a new job and while enthusiasm to Richard was a deceitful, potentially dangerous state of being, for once he couldn't suppress it. He hadn't been able to shake the wide grin he'd had since getting up, and though it used muscles that normally lay dormant, it was simply beyond his control. For once in his life he was going to let himself enjoy the moment and if jaw ache, cracked cheekbones, or a potential change of wind direction led to permanent grinning idiot status, then bring it on.

Something crackled behind him, footsteps on the gravel perhaps, and there was a muffled voice giving someone a dressing down. Pretending he hadn't heard it, he bent to move the large metallic flight case at his feet, the dozens of red FRAGILE stickers on it making him think twice about touching the thing at all. There was another crackle and more muffled exhortations, and this time he stood, rubbing his neck, leaving the fragile coffin-sized strongbox glowing in the rising sun as though it were possessed. He turned around but saw nothing as the dawn sun reflected off one of the dozens of windows opposite him. Then the crackle came again, still from behind him though, and he realised it was the walkie-talkie in his back pocket, and the impatient, hectoring voice was that of his friend of uncertain status and secret object of desire, the highly demanding, Valérie d'Orçay. Glamorous and exotic, she blinded Richard like the sun on the windows. She was also his new business partner, though in truth the word 'partner' was doing an awful lot of heavy lifting in that description. By trade, Valérie was a professional bounty hunter and possible assassin of international repute, while Richard was a maker of tourist breakfasts and a former film historian. He was also of international repute; he had a doctorate to prove it, though it was of little use in their new business of Private Investigators and Personal Security. It had been her idea and he had, naturally, gone along with it.

He plucked the walkie-talkie from his back pocket and replied to the snappy crackles. 'Yes, Richard here. Over.'

'Over what?' was the testy reply.

'No. Over. You say over when you're... over.'

There was a pause and he suspected a deep breath had got lost somewhere in the ether. 'I did not know you had used a talkie-walkie before.' She was trying to sound patient while at the same time letting him know who was really in charge. Also she'd used the word 'talkie-walkie' which was French for walkie-talkie, one of those peculiarities of the French language where they had taken an internationally recognised word yet still tried to retain control over it. Either way, talkie-walkie was a very pleasing twist.

'We'll be over in twenty minutes,' she said seriously.

'No, you put the over at the end,' he joked, immediately regretting it. In the past few months they had spent a lot of time together and still Richard hadn't been able to eradicate flippancy or sarcasm from his conversation – two things that usually flew straight over Valérie's head, like a perfectly executed tennis lob.

'Richard?' she crackled again, the crackle not all atmospheric. 'We shall be with you in twenty minutes.'

'I'll be here,' he replied seriously and he heard the radio go dead.

He sat down on the big flight case wondering what to do in the next twenty minutes that would indicate to the imminent Valérie that he'd done anything at all. It wasn't actually his responsibility to be moving the flight case, he just felt like he should do something. It was dawn, there were very few other people about, but he really should make an effort. After reappraising the size of the case, however, and the fact that its four wheels meant nothing on the gravel beneath them, he decided to sit and rest instead for the next eighteen minutes at least. Keep an eye on things. As nominal Head of Security, it was the least he could do.

Sitting on the case he turned again to the sight of the slowly rising sun reflected in the windows and the ornamental pond that stood between him and the west wing of the magnificent Chateau de Valençay. From where he sat, he could see the three main stages of its construction: the Gallo-Roman, the Renaissance and the Enlightenment; the two great domes on its west wing loomed large in the dawn light. The chateau smacked of wealth and power, of opulence and riches, of political intrigue and history-defining moments stretching back nearly a thousand years. He liked that; he wasn't one for the supernatural but to him it gave off an energy. What was it Orson Welles said about the Borgias in *The Third Man*? For thirty years they had warfare, terror and bloodshed and produced the Renaissance, while in Switzerland they had five hundred years of brotherly love and produced the cuckoo clock. Richard sighed. He felt a bit under pressure knowing that the Chateau de Valençay, itself the result of warfare, terror and bloodshed was, for the next twenty minutes or so, solely his responsibility. He'd have preferred to guard a cuckoo clock.

He gulped nervously just as a peacock somewhere in the manicured gardens woke and began its morning squawk. It sounded mocking to Richard, another sign of the other-worldly luxury of the place, and he missed his calmer, less brash hens. What right had he to be Head of Security for the Chateau de Valençay anyway? This really hadn't been in his mind at all when Valérie had first mooted the idea of a detective agency. They had had two prior adventures, cases, investigations – he wasn't sure what to call them – but he had been very much dragged along in Valérie's tempest of a wake, for the most part happy to hang on to her impeccable coat-tails and just, really, to be with the woman who was as intoxicating, mysterious and enchanting as the waking chateau he was guarding.

They had had a few enquiries for business initially, but they were all to do with marital infidelity which, while it got their business off to a flying start financially, was also beginning to lose Richard drinking partners in the local bar and gain him stony looks in the market. They had swiftly rebranded to say that they didn't do 'marital' work and the Follet Valley, worried about the fallout, had breathed a collective sigh of relief. Business had been quiet since then until this job came in, and though not strictly within the boundary of the Follet Valley itself, Valençay was close enough to be local. This job now had Richard guarding a thousand years of French and European history, and a few hundred thousand euros of film equipment ready for the production of *The Master Servant*, a new Hollywood blockbuster. At the same time Valérie was personal security and bodyguard to one of its main stars, the fragile, beautiful Lionel Margaux, who was playing Napoleon's second wife, Marie-Louise of Austria.

It had been at Lionel Margaux's request that Valérie, and nominally Richard, become her personal bodyguards and on-set security. Her mother and Valérie were friends, and when the young Lionel Margaux had become the victim of a stalker while filming in Paris, it was decided that the production would move to Valençay, at great expense too, though with a smaller crew. This film was a Franco-American production, the actress representing the best of the Franco part, so money was no object. Besides, the publicity department had said, what could be better than filming the interior scenes where they had historically taken place?

Richard looked at his watch and wondered if he should just take a look around the courtyard and the entrance bridge that came over the long-dried moat, check for snipers or something. Do stalkers use snipers? Do snipers use stalkers even? He had no idea but he should take a quick look anyway and tip-toed, for no good reason, through the central welcoming arch under the keep. It was all eerily quiet, even the gargoyles seemed half asleep, and he turned and went back the other way, where he'd come from, past the pond in the *Cour d'Honneur* and out towards the *Jardin de la Duchesse* which had, in the daytime anyway, a magnificent view over this side of the valley.

He descended the stone steps into the garden and for the first time felt tense. The two statues in each of the symmetrical flower beds were half-lit by the morning sun and it made them look threatening. Richard tightened the grip on his heavy torch, trying not to focus on the fact that if a couple of statues were giving him the shivers, a potentially murderous stalker was probably not his department at all, and maybe in future he should offer to stick to the admin side of the business.

'You there!' The voice was deep and immediately authoritative, stopping Richard in his tracks. The clipped English tones were slightly softened with a continental edge, but that didn't detract from the voice, and presumably the person behind it, being very used to power and to wielding it. 'What do you think you're doing, prowling around my gardens at this time of day, eh? I should have you thrashed!'

Richard turned slowly as a man emerged from the shadows behind the stone steps, a pronounced limp making his movements look laboured.

'Well? Explain yourself, monsieur!'

The aristocratic bearing and even the language were early nineteenth century, the powdered wig the same; but the low-slung jogging bottoms and trainers were definitely not period, and for a moment Richard thought he'd chanced on the stalker. A nutcase with an Enlightenment fetish and a leisurewear addiction.

'The emperor arrives today, man. I won't have strangers cluttering up my gardens!'

The man kept coming at his slow, debilitated pace. Of medium to small height, the wig high on his forehead, his skin was pale, and though smaller than Richard, his air of authority made it feel like he was taller. Then Richard almost dropped his torch. This wasn't a stalker at all, this was Dominic Burdett, Hollywood star since he was eight years old and one of the great movie actors of his generation. His commitment to his roles bordered famously on dangerous obsession as his method acting had at times brought him close to breakdown with drastic changes in weight and punishing, sometimes dangerous research, all in the name of his art. So while this wasn't a stalker, in an odd way it wasn't Dominic Burdett either. This was, to all intents and purposes, His Serene Highness Prince Charles-Maurice de Talleyrand-Périgord, owner of the Chateau de Valençay and the subject of the film itself. Burdett was in character, leisurewear notwithstanding.

Back up the steps Richard heard a motorbike come loudly through the keep arch and skid to a halt in the gravel. *Dammit*, he thought, *that's where I should be!* And he ran halfway up the steps before stopping and turning back to the figure below. 'Er,' he said, 'excuse me, Your Grace.' And continued with haste to the courtyard.

A motorbike with two riders had stopped right in front of the set entrance, and Richard's heart beat faster. Both riders wore heavy biker leathers and still had their helmets on, classic modern assassin get-up he decided, basing his conclusion on nothing more than something he'd read somewhere. Should he approach them? I mean, it was his job after all. But if his instincts were right, his job didn't, as far as he was aware, entail martyrdom.

'Erm, excuse me, but you can't bring that bike in here.' As a confrontational opening gambit towards two potentially desperate killers, it left something to be desired, and he regretted his actions as the lead rider slowly started to remove their helmet.

'Ooh, you're scary! Change of plan, didn't madame tell you?' The redoubtable Madame Tablier, his long-time cleaning woman, scourge of germs and social niceties, looked around her. 'I wouldn't want to have to clean all those windows,' she said as Richard let out a sigh of relief. Then the pillion passenger shakily removed their helmet too and shook her long blonde hair. Lionel Margaux, the hottest name in French cinema, though with a haunted, delicate fear about her. A fragility that was almost transparent.

She looked at Richard, terror in her eyes. 'I never want to go on a motorcycle ever again!' she said, on the verge of tears. 'I think I'd rather live with a stalker.'

'Well!' Madame Tablier huffed. 'That's gratitude for you!'

Coming soon

Death at the Chateau
(A Follet Valley Mystery 3)

Richard Ainsworth and Valérie d'Orçay have set up their detective agency and after eschewing all 'marital work', to avoid being ostracised by French society, they now have their first assignment. They are to protect beautiful actress Lionel Margaux as she works on a Franco-American film production in the nearby Chateau de Valençay.

Richard's first day on the job starts badly when a Resistance hero dies on set and despite all the evidence pointing to natural causes, Richard tries to convince a sceptical Valérie otherwise. But when major American film star Reed Turnbull also dies in mysterious circumstances, they both know there's definitely a murderer in the crew.

PRE-ORDER NOW!

Also available

Death and Fromage
(A Follet Valley Mystery 2)

Richard is a middle-aged Englishman who runs a B&B in the Val de Follet. Nothing ever happens to Richard, and really that's the way he likes it.

Until scandal erupts in the nearby town of Saint-Sauver when its famous restaurant is downgraded from three 'Michelin' stars to two. The restaurant is shamed, the town is in shock and the leading goat's cheese supplier drowns himself in one of his own pasteurisation tanks. Or does he?

Valérie d'Orçay, who is staying at the B&B while house-hunting in the area, isn't convinced that it's a suicide. Despite his misgivings, Richard is drawn into Valérie's investigation, and finds himself becoming a major player.

OUT NOW

About the Author

Credit: Richard Wood

Ian Moore is a leading stand-up comedian, known for his sharp, entertaining punditry. He has performed all over the world, on every continent except South America. A TV/radio regular, he stars in Dave's satirical TV show *Unspun* and Channel 5's topical comedy *Big Mouths*.

Ian lives in rural France and commutes back to the UK every week. In his spare time, he makes mean chutneys and jams.

Note from the Publisher

To receive background material and updates on further humorous titles by Ian Moore, sign up at farragobooks.com/ian-moore-signup